# Mount of Hope:
# A Victorian Tale of Young Love

Jamie Michele
&
Mrs. Trollope

Vintage Volumes

**Mount of Hope:**
**A Victorian Tale of Young Love**

ISBN-13: 978-0692440797 (Vintage Volumes)
ISBN-10: 0692440798

For Mom.

With all my heart,
I wish you were still here to read this.

And yet,
somehow,
I know you are.

Dearest Reader,

If you would be so kind as to permit me, I should like to tell you something before you begin your journey back to 19th century England. What I mean to say, dear reader, is that you are not being ushered back to a bygone era by a 21st century storyteller. You are, in fact, about to embark on a tale of Victorian love, written by a Victorian author—during the Victorian era—for her Victorian readers.

In short, dear reader, the unabridged, original version of this book was published in 1844 as Mrs. Trollope's Young Love. It was sold in three lovely volumes and totaled an impressive 1,064 pages before, alas, it went out of print.

Having acquired these facts, you might now be asking—who, then, are *you*? I, esteemed reader, am the 21st century author who endeavored to abridge and rework this piece of forgotten 19th century literature. I did so with the greatest hope that, perhaps, the language and length of this redraft might prove more accessible to contemporary readers. As a custodian of her manuscript, I took special care to keep Mrs. Trollope's lyrical style and omniscient point of view largely intact.

And with that, dear reader, I must leave you to enjoy Mount of Hope: A Victorian Tale of Young Love, and beg to subscribe myself,
   Your dutiful and humble scribe,
   Jamie Michele

# Prologue

Happy is the man who, wishing to live and die in the bliss of country greatness, has his acres situated in a neighborhood where there is no nobleman's seat to be seen.

Colonel William Henry Dermont of the Mount was a happy man. For, in this essential particular, he was blessed beyond the common lot of English country gentlemen, having no duke, marquis, earl, viscount, baron, baronet—not even a knight—within many miles of him. With a snug wooded estate producing easy rents of nearly four thousand a year, he knew himself to be the greatest man in the neighborhood.

The Mount was situated in the parish of Stoke; a comfortable, pretty place with plenty of wood, water, and every suitable accommodation for a family possessed of the Dermont revenues. The soil was kindly, and grateful for the care bestowed upon it, producing good returns of corn and butter, fruit and flowers.

Neither Colonel Dermont nor his wife wished for more. They were of that happily born class of people who are inclined to think that everything they possess is a good deal better than anything of the same possessed by anyone else. In no degree could they be considered unusually stately in their demeanor, or in any way overbearing in the consciousness of their superiority. The very worst that could be said of them was that they were aware of their many advantages. It must be an ill tempered being who could find fault in them with this.

They had been married six years and had but one child, a boy. He was thought to be exceedingly handsome and intelligent, although at times a little headstrong—which his nurse thought might be owing to his being rather indulged more than other children. She also thought his generous and affectionate nature atoned for his occasional naughtiness.

Their want of a daughter was, by some degree, supplied by the presence of a little orphan girl who had been thrown upon their protection under the most honorable of circumstances.

In Colonel Dermont's younger years he had insisted, like a good many other young men, upon being permitted to put on a red coat. His parents conceded reluctantly and to India he went. He most assuredly would never have lived to come back again had it not been for the timely aid of a brother officer, who galloped to his side exactly in time to save his life.

Major Drummond, the gallant officer who performed this service for him, did not survive it long. A wound received in the same action caused his death after a lingering confinement of four months. Upon his death, Colonel Dermont attended to Major Drummond's widow and young daughter, escorting them home to England.

Colonel Dermont married within a few months of his return to England, the early loss of both his parents having put him in possession of his estate. Four years after their marriage, the sudden death of Major Drummond's daughter in childbirth—her husband and mother already in their graves—resulted in the orphan baby girl being consigned to the guardianship of Colonel Dermont and his kind wife.

Little baby Julia was brought to the Mount and the nursery establishment for the two children was the same as if they had been the offspring of the same parents. Never had Colonel Dermont forgotten his moment of peril, in which the arm of his little ward's gallant grandfather saved his life. But, notwithstanding these sentiments, they could neither of them forget that the fine, noble looking child Alfred was their own, and that little Julia was not. This distinction did not injure the girl or interfere with her happiness. She was as content as the petted dog Bingo himself, and was of little more consequence than he. This conviction brought no pain with it, nor ever caused her for a moment to wish to be as important a personage as Alfred. Even in the moments when he was most indulged, she did not wish to change places with him. She was a quick little thing and of so gay a temperament, she made up her mind that though she was only a girl, she was the best off of the two—permitted to trot here and there, while the idolized Alfred was watched every moment of the day. It was as if the welfare of the universe depended on his not being too hot or too cold, too fasting or too fed, too much in movement or at rest.

As to Alfred himself, he was by no means dull enough not to perceive how remarkably exalted a place he occupied. By the time he was eight years old, he was fully aware that there was nobody in the house of so much importance as himself.

Colonel and Mrs. Dermont were highly respected and liked in the neighborhood, and the Dermonts in return appeared to have a great regard for almost everybody. They never gave less than two handsome dinners every month, accommodating the principle members of about half a dozen families who lived too far to conveniently return home after dinner. These were the duties of hospitality which they thought too great a sin to omit.

Guests heartily agreed that the dinners were as well prepared as those beyond their reach in London and Paris could be. There was a pianoforte always in tolerable tune for the use of young ladies, when they were of the singing and playing class. There were always two Books of Beauty of the current year on the drawing room table, and in winter there was always a good fire— in summer an abundance of flowers. And, of course, there was always Alfred to be looked at.

The preparations for staying were equally perfect and rarely lasted less than three full days. Mrs. Dermont herself would accompany each lady guest to her chamber when she retired to make her toilet for dinner. She reminded ladies where the bell was that would bring her maid with hot water. On these occasions she never failed to say, "You must not give yourself any trouble dressing today. We shall have nobody but our good clergyman, but tomorrow, we hope to get some friends to meet you."

On day two the young ladies were recommended, weather permitting, to walk in the shade of the woods as there were no rough paths to encounter. Older ladies were invited to look at the conservatory. For the gentlemen, both young and old, there were fishing rods in spring and summer, guns and shuttlecock in the autumn and winter, and the billiard table all year round.

On day three both Colonel and Mrs. Dermont would declare that their guests must not think of leaving, for their kind neighbors the *A's* and *B's* (and, if it was fine, the *C's* and *D's* also) would be joining in the evening, and perhaps they might get up a little dance or play charades. Moreover, Alfred had been promised that he could stay up as long as he liked, and so they positively must not go. All this was done with such kindness, that it was quite impossible not to declare the Dermonts the most delightful people in the world.

This routine went on with wonderful regularity for many years and Alfred mixed himself with the guests, sometimes with words and smiles, sometimes with cuffs and kicks. When the latter occurred, those who were sufficiently intimate with the family were aware that great relief might be obtained by employing the agency of little Julia. A good deal of familiarity with the interior of the establishment was required to learn this, as the diminutive and odd looking girl elicited little notice from anyone. Colonel and Mrs. Dermont knew the child was perfectly well and perfectly happy, and did not feel it necessary to drag her forward to notice.

Little Julia was constantly overlooked as there was really very little about her to attract an unobservant eye. She was not ugly, but most assuredly she was not pretty. Her features were small and her colorless complexion was devoid of the freshness so charming in children. Her pretty-enough little eyebrows and the size and shape of her richly lashed ebony eyes were in no way assisted by thick, coal black hair that would not part properly in front. The most marked observation that had been uttered upon her appearance was by a lively young lady who declared, "I have never seen another little creature so completely black and white!"

Her nurse was wont to say that she was a sharp little pin with a raven black head, however, the sharpness in which her nurse alluded was to Julia's quickness of intellect. Alfred Dermont was nearly four years older than Julia Drummond, but their education went on together. When Alfred turned six, a governess was engaged to whom both children were consigned as pupils. If the education of Julia threatened to be prematurely advanced, Alfred appeared decidedly the reverse. His bright blue eyes had never been forced to fix themselves on the letters of the alphabet, a shock to the governess not lessened by him saying coolly, "I think you are a very ugly person, Miss Harding. I think your lesson is a very stupid lesson, and if you ever tell me to do it again I will kick you. Come along, Julia!"

Miss Harding had released a gentle sigh and watched the children run off, sitting immovably in the place they left her, in deep consideration of the ways and means that would be necessary for her to resort.

It is needless to follow up the patient labors of Miss Harding as it was achieved at last, with assistance the governess derived from Julia. At age two she had spoken with perfect distinction. Before the age of four she could read any book set before her. Master Alfred eventually followed her example, with little more to be said until a dozen long years passed over their eight and four year old heads.

# Chapter 1

At twenty years old, Alfred Dermont was certainly a handsome young man. He stood over six feet, his features were magnificent, and had his countenance expressed a little less daring self confidence—it might have been charming. His large blue eyes were framed with brows that frequently arched to suggest his contempt for those around him, and his smile, though too often timed to be most impertinent, displayed teeth of perfection.

Alfred's education had been strangely irregular. He certainly was not ignorant, and yet he could scarcely be said to be thoroughly well informed on any subject—for his studies rarely went beyond the point to which his inclination led him, and the moment he ceased to be amused, he ceased to continue studying. At age twelve there had been a great deal of half-hearted talk about sending him to Eton. But his father confessed to his mother, and his mother confessed to his father, that they could not part with him. Having separately and conjointly come to this decision, they determined, like sensible people, to act upon it.

Act upon it they did, and Alfred Dermont never left his paternal roof, either for school or college. Instead, tutors of English, French, and German were bestowed on him liberally; and as the boy was quick and some of the tutors quite clever, the result was a patchwork education. Some portions were brilliant and effective, others were a good deal the reverse.

As to Julia, Colonel Dermont continued steadfast in his resolution that not a single shilling of the seven thousand pound inheritance she was to receive at the age of majority—bequeathed to her in trust by Major Drummond and his descendant—neither principle nor interest, should ever be expended on her until she choose to expend it herself.

The home education of Alfred was an expensive one, for it included horses, dogs, and a town built cab for the younger gentleman's own particular driving. His collection of books was continually increasing in the variety of languages he was taught. The colonel observed to his wife that when Miss Harding went, there could be no objection to Julia's taking lessons with Alfred as she had always done. Little Julia, nor her friend Alfred, nor any of the learned professors concerned made any objection to the arrangement. The usual feminine accomplishments of music and drawing were left out, but Julia became possessed of a larger portion of information than would generally fall on most young ladies.

At sixteen Julia was still a queer looking little creature, so much so, that nobody thought it civil to discuss her appearance. As her intellectual acquirements were utterly unknown there was nothing to redeem her from the sort of easy oblivion which seemed to be her fate. But never did a happier creature exist on God's earth. Her health was excellent and her spirits were high. She learned all that was set before her with equal facility and correctness, and she never for an instant made herself, her situation, her accomplishments, or her person the subject of her own thoughts. She lived in a state of the most delightful unconsciousness as to her own insignificance.

Good Colonel Dermont, when soothing himself as he occasionally did, by boasting that he had given Julia Drummond an excellent education, never guessed how excellent it actually had been. He didn't know he had annihilated in the heart of his ward the most fatal weakness that can beset a person. Still less perhaps, he did not guess that while conferring this benefit upon her, he was overwhelming his son by fostering and cherishing in him the identical mental malady from which she had so happily escaped. Nevertheless, it did not follow that because Julia Drummond was free from all illusions of self love, she was free likewise from all illusions likely to arise from love to others. As such, Julia loved and admired Alfred even more blindly than own his parents. Far different was the condition of Alfred. Though brought up side by side, and receiving what a superficial observer might call the same education, a single moral ingredient was rendered differently and the result was in great contrast to Julia's. Alfred truly, simply, and sincerely believed himself to be one of the most glorious specimens of humanity. He was so firmly convinced of the necessity of having his own way that many good gifts were destroyed by it.

"What a delightful summer we seem likely to have," said Mrs. Dermont. She stood next to her husband and admired the vast lawn before them. "Don't you think it would be a good scheme if this fine weather lasts, to invite the whole neighborhood together to breakfast on the lawn? Music and dancing—I think it would please Alfred. Yesterday he said he wished there was a bit more variety in our parties. He said it quite seriously."

The colonel looked at his wife with interest. "Did he? Then I'm sure we ought to manage to get a little more variety, and a dance on the lawn would be quite new. But how shall we get enough young men together? Ladies cannot dance without gentlemen, you know."

"There is but one way, my dear husband. You must ask the officers quartered at Overby, *en masse*. People of consequence in a neighborhood very often do that without having any personal introduction at all."

"Yes, I know they do and I have no objection, if Alfred approves it. It will lead to no great danger of making disagreeable acquaintance, for I dare say they will be sent off again as soon as the talk of riots is over. Alfred and I can ride to Overby and speak to Major Sommerton about it. He is an old acquaintance and would let me know if there was any objection."

The colonel looked past the lawn to the flowers, his hands over his eyes to shield them from the sun. "Where is Alfred? Of course we must not decide upon it until we have asked him. Have you seen him since breakfast? I looked for him in the library but he was not there. Have you seen him?"

"I saw him within this half hour, walking away towards the wilderness with a book in his hand. What an extraordinary creature he is, to be sure! He certainly takes pleasure in reading, even now that his education is so completely finished as to render it quite unnecessary. An extraordinary young man!"

"Extraordinary in every way!" replied the colonel. "But if he is gone to the wilderness, let us go there too and speak to him about this scheme of yours." He offered his arm to his wife.

They walked a ways in the shade of their well kept shrubbery—nicknamed the wilderness—and saw at a distance their son seated on a bench with the book still in his hand. Julia stood before him, whether listening to his reading or only looking at him, they could not tell.

Mrs. Dermont paused with her husband for a moment to gaze upon her son. "What a graceful lounging position he has chosen colonel, hasn't he?"

He yielded to the pressure his wife placed on his arm to restrain his steps. "I will not deny it. He certainly is the finest fellow of his age that I ever looked at."

"Yes, my dear, but what a blessing it is that Julia is so plain! Don't you see how constantly they are together? If she were at all well looking or particularly striking in any way, I should be frightened to death lest he should take it into his head to fall in love with her. But, thank goodness there is no danger of that!"

"It is quite well perhaps that Julia should be plain as handsome, because it sets your mind, and maybe my own too, at rest upon that matter. But between ourselves wife, Alfred is not a young man to throw his heart away upon any girl who had nothing better to distinguish her than a pretty face. Alfred has an immense deal of pride, and you may take my word for it, he will never make any matrimonial connection that will not satisfy us in every way. I would trust his judgment in all ways."

"I think so too, colonel."

Mrs. Dermont propelled her husband's footsteps as gently and effectively as she had done before. In a matter of minutes, they stood beside their son with four fond eyes fixed earnestly upon him.

Colonel Dermont rested his hands on the young man's shoulder. "We have followed you to your literary retreat Alfred, in order to consult you about a little party that your mother is proposing to give. Might you put your book down for a moment to hear about it?"

"Here Julia, take the book. I have had quite enough of it." He put the novel into the hands of his companion. "Now then ma'am, what is it you have to say?"

"Do you think you might make room for us, Alfred? It is really too hot for anybody to stand."

Alfred moved his long limbs to only occupy a third of the seat. His parents placed themselves beside him, Julia still maintaining her standing position in front.

Nothing could be further from the heart of either the colonel or his wife than an uncivil feeling toward their young ward, but the negligence towards her was so habitual as to render it nearly impossible that they should treat her otherwise than as a mere child—towards which anything approaching ceremony would be ridiculous.

There were moments in which young Alfred appeared to be under the influence of the same view, but nevertheless, seeing there was no room for her on the bench, he got up. He made slow, deliberate, and rather languid steps the distance of about a hundred yards to a tree, under which there was a movable mushroom seat. He passed a slender finger through the aperture at its top and brought it to the spot where the group was assembled. He then replaced himself on the bench and, having done so, made a silent sign for Julia to take possession of it. She did so with a glance of gratitude towards her friend.

Mrs. Dermont smiled. "Upon my word Miss Julia, I think you are highly honored."

The slightest of frowns passed over the brow of Alfred. "Well ma'am, what is it you have got to tell me?"

"Why Alfred, you see my dear, the weather is most beautifully fine. I have been thinking that, by way of making a little variety and trying something new in the manner of receiving our neighbors, we might, if you like my dear, give something of a dance upon the lawn. Something in the way of a breakfast. What do you say, Alfred?"

"Oh dear, ma'am, I have no objection whatsoever, provided you can get together people enough. But our lawns are large and it will be a very forlorn looking business if the groups are too thinly scattered. Should you like it, Julia?"

Both the colonel and Mrs. Dermont felt this question to be rather an idle interruption in a discussion of so interesting a subject, but as it came from Alfred, they paused until the answer was given. It did not take long.

"Like it? To be sure I should! I should think it would be the most beautiful thing in the world! People dancing upon the lawn—oh, lovely!"

"Well, well, no doubt of it," said Mrs. Dermont. "And now let us think a little about numbers, Alfred. You must know it is a point that puzzles the colonel and I."

Alfred released a sigh. "Unfortunately the people here, for the most part, are horrible bores. And the women are almost all of them ugly."

The colonel smiled and held up his finger. "All of them, Alfred? Have you forgotten the beautiful Miss Thorwold?"

Alfred colored slightly. "I have not forgotten her, but I did not know whether she might be gone before the party. She is only on a visit, you know. If she were to be here—"

"She is to stay the whole year, my dear, I can tell you," said his mother. "Her uncle, Lord Ripley, is to take her to town with him when the parliament meets after Christmas. Then as to numbers, we must do as all country people are obliged to do when they give a *fete champetre*—we must invite all the best of Overby people! And as there is no help for it, we must ask the Overby townspeople as well."

"We can do so on such an occasion as this without the slightest impropriety," said the colonel. "It will not do as a general practice, for country families to make much visiting with the country town people. It would be breaking down all distinction. But at a great gathering, such as a christening or coming of age, you hear, or anything of that sort, all the first nobility invite the people of their country town. *Fete champetre* invitations may be quite as general, without giving occasion to any disagreeable observations whatsoever. Yes, certainly, we must ask the Overby people."

Julia was listening with great attention. "I wish you would tell me ma'am, what is the reason people that live in a country town are not thought fit to visit the people that live outside the town? I am sure that some of the town children that Alfred and I used to meet at the dancing school at Overby were the best scholars Mr Laman had. And some of them were so pretty and good natured."

Colonel Dermont fell into the philosophical tone he sometimes did when addressing sensitive matters. "There is no reason in the world, Julia, no reason whatsoever, my dear, why children of persons living in a country town should not be pretty and good natured. But you must remember, my dear child, that it is the duty of the higher classes to keep up the distinctions which it has pleased Providence to make. Gentlemen residing on their estates in the country are quite a different class of people from those who live in the country towns. Perhaps you cannot, as yet, fully understand this."

"Oh yes! I know all about the difference that riches, high birth, and good education make, and that it is a mischievous idea to suppose all people in the world would be happier if these distinctions were removed. God himself has made men different in their dispositions, or as to their powers, so that they must be in different situations. Miss Harding and Mr. Brown too, used to explain all that to us. Alfred and I both understood it well. But it does not seem to me that the impossibility of the country gentlemen visiting the town gentlemen has anything to do with that."

"Of course, my dear little girl, you have only learned the great general rules of an organized society, as yet. It requires a longer acquaintance with life to fully understand what may be called the special regulations of the different classes. But we are too busy for me to enter upon any such explanation just at present. Yet even the business before us, my dear, will give you an opportunity of remarking that there is no want of liberality in *our* notions on the subject. I am clearly of the opinion, Alfred, that we may venture to invite poor, good Major Murray's two daughters. You know we have had them here repeatedly, and then there is the widow of the late vicar, and her pretty daughter. And if your mother does not object to it, I really don't see why we should not invite Mr., Mrs., and Miss Kersley and the young attorney—the son, I mean—not the other young man who is articled to Mr. Kersley. I don't know anything about him. Kersley himself is an exceedingly respectable person and has dined here already, as you know, over and over again."

"I shall have no objection whatsoever," replied Mrs. Dermont. "They are very decent people, all of them—decent, well behaved people."

Alfred raised his eyebrows. "Decent? My dear mother, that phrase does not seem to promise much for the elegance of your party."

Julia looked earnestly into the face of Mrs. Dermont. "I wish you could tell me the real meaning of the word decent, ma'am."

"It has more meanings than one, my dear Julia," replied Mrs. Dermont. "What I mean by it at present is that the Kersleys are well looking, well dressed sorts of people, and perfectly respectable in character."

"Not like that second son of Mr. Fitzwarrington, of Warrington Park," said Julia, nodding her head. "I understand."

Alfred laughed. "What an impertinent little thing you are, Julia."

"What does she mean, Alfred?" asked the colonel.

Alfred laughed again. "I suspect, sir, that she is alluding to the story she heard Mrs. Beaumont tell the other day, about William Fitzwarrington's having won that horse race unfairly. I dare say Julia does not think that decent at all!"

Mrs. Dermont looked grave. "That is a foolish play on words, my dear. It is all very well to make jokes when there is no business going on, but now we really are busy, so pray, do not interrupt us with anymore nonsense. If this party is to be given, we must not waste time, I assure you."

"We shall do nothing, mother, without pen, ink, and paper," said Alfred, rising. "So I vote we adjourn to the library."

His suggestion was immediately complied with, and to the library they went. Alfred led the way, his father and mother following, and Julia coming after in obedience to a signal from the young man.

"Sit down Julia, and write the names as we call them over," said Mrs. Dermont. "That is what Alfred says ought to be done first."

Julia obeyed, and a list was soon produced.

Mrs. Dermont looked it over. "I had no idea there were so many people in the neighborhood."

"It always turns out so, my dear, when one sets about gathering people together. I supposed Julia is to be secretary in producing the invitations," said the colonel. "While this is going on, Alfred and I had better ride to Overby and make a few inquiries of Major Sommerton. I believe the young officers are still quartered at Overby."

Alfred curled his lip at the notion of inviting the red coats *en masse*, but his mother remarked with a sigh, "Disagreeable as this certainly is, it will be impossible to get up a tolerable dancing party without them."

After indulging in another sneer, Alfred assured his mother that he did not seriously mean to oppose it. "Of course you must write the notes, Julia," he said, leaving the library. "But take care not to forget the hole in the fishing net you were to mend for me. It is possible I may want it tomorrow."

Julia promised speed on both the notes and fishing net, and kept her word. All was done before the gentlemen returned from their ride.

# Chapter 2

Such an invitation from the Mount was not likely to be met in any quarter by a refusal. When the replies had all been counted, it became rather evident that there was no room in the house which would permit the whole party to sit down together to a banquet.

The drawing room might have permitted a double row of tables, each long enough to accommodate about forty persons. However, when this was suggested by Julia and Alfred, the colonel and his lady both started as if a bucket of cold water had been thrown over them. The notion of introducing a great meal with all the accompaniments of flying champagne corks and spilling of claret, having all this in the most elegant drawing room in the county was inconceivable.

Mrs. Dermont exchanged a worried glance with the colonel. "It is no good to joke about it, dear Alfred and Julia. We very seriously must contrive some plan or other by which all the ladies, at the very least, might be accommodated with seats.

Colonel Dermont came to the rescue of his wife. "I will tell you what we must do, and I only wonder that it did not occur to me sooner. We might request to borrow a marquee from Major Sommerton, and one or two others from Captain Waters or Captain Smith. Nothing looks so gay and picturesque as tents pitched upon a lawn. With the military band stationed along the trees to the left, the effect will be beautiful."

All four agreed it was a clever idea indeed, and another ride was immediately planned for the two gentlemen to Overby.

Even if Colonel Dermont had not been *the* Colonel Dermont, who had so much distinguished himself in India as to have been very nearly killed, Major Sommerton would have been only too happy to do all they could to promote so very agreeable a scheme. The tents and music were easily secured.

Preparations for the fete began with great activity in almost every part of the grounds and mansion at the Mount. All the male servants, with the colonel and Alfred to assist them, were employed in erecting upon the lawn three tents. Julia, with Mrs. Dermont's maid to help, was working on making wreaths to hang about the white drapery of the tents. With marvelous skill and the aid of wire, she converted unnumbered yards of calico, white, pink, blue, yellow and crimson into roses and lilies to be combined with an abundance of evergreens.

The housekeeper, the cook, and the scullion labored from morning to night, producing every imaginable variety of sweet and savory delicacies. The dairy maid procured and preserved incredible quantities of cream. The gardener was protecting his ripe strawberries from the sun. The butler's pantry was locked to secure the plate which had undergone a good polishing. There was no corner of the establishment that was not involved in preparation.

One of the male servants working on the lawn caught sight of the carriage of Mr. Stephens as it approached the house. He darted off, catching up his livery coat as he ran towards the house. Out of breath, but in a style still befitting the dignity of the Mount, he announced, "Mr. And Mrs. Stephens!"

Mrs. Dermont was found sitting in her drawing room, looking ladylike and idle. It was, in her estimation, possible for the Mount to produce a magnificent fete without degrading the elegant repose of its mistress.

Mrs. Dermont had not quite made up her mind whether to like or dislike the newly arrived Mr. and Mrs. Stephens of Beech Hill. She greatly approved of their moving the old posts from the lawn and replacing them with a light and neat iron fence. She did not, however, quite like the free and easy style in which Mrs. Stephens overhauled neatly bound books upon the drawing room table, stating in a patronizing tone that if any in the family were readers, they should be perfectly welcome to dip into the treasures of Mr. Stephens' library. There was something in the notion that the family at the Mount might want to borrow anything of anybody which grated on Mrs. Dermont's feelings. There was also something much like a tone of equality in Mr. Stephens' manner of saying they would wait until the smell of paint had left the dining room to fix a day for hosting the Mount family, as if he was perfectly certain the family would go wherever they were asked. But then, Mr. Stephens' manner of expressing his admiration of the house, grounds, and various other parts and parcels of the Mount was so very gentlemanly and pleasing, she felt it impossible to doubt his having been good company.

Mr. and Mrs. Stephens, and their rather odd looking friend, entered—the very picture of elegant repose, though every other individual in the house was in a bustle.

Mrs. Dermont was not one who thought it proper to shake hands with everybody, but she graciously gave the tips of four fingers to Mrs. Stephens, and her whole hand to Mr. Stephens. Mr. Stephens announced their friend as Mr. Holingsworth. As was polite, Mr. Stephens and Mr. Holingsworth walked to a distant window to admire the fine trees and green grass which grew under them, while Mrs. Stephens drew a chair close to the sofa on which the lady of the house was seated.

"It is probable, my dear Mrs. Dermont, that you are not yet acquainted with the name of Holingsworth. He has, in fact, but recently arrived in England. I should really feel wanting in duty to myself, to you, to the colonel, and to your highly gifted son if I failed to make you acquainted with him. He is one of the most celebrated men who have visited England from New York for many years. His principle object in visiting the country is to observe and experience the general tone of manners of the English aristocracy, before he publishes his great work of society throughout Europe. Can you wonder, my dear lady, that knowing this we should be so anxious to bring him here? We should be delighted to obtain permission for him to be present at your fete on Thursday. Above all, we should be deeply anxious that he should not leave Stoke without having been introduced to your son."

Mrs. Dermont, though a good deal inclined to be stiff to new people in general, relaxed at once on hearing the pleas of Mrs. Stephens to meet her son. "Both the colonel and myself would be happy to see the gentleman with you on Thursday."

Mrs. Stephens smiled in relief. "Well then, with that settled, we must now take our leave. Our next duty is to show our distinguished traveler the magnificent view of the Colonel's house and grounds as seen from the upper road to Overby."

# Chapter 3

The important day arrived bright in sunshine, with scarcely wind enough to wave the lightest of a lady's ringlet. The hour appointed by the invitation for assembling was two, and before half an hour beyond it had worn itself away, the lawn at the Mount was full.

There were, as there always must be at English gatherings, many pretty young women. The red coats from Overby illuminated various groups, the presence of the military professionals being both useful and ornamental in the highest degree. The officers were greatly pleased to see the Oswalds and the Fitzwarringtons arrive, giving them opportunity to improve their acquaintance. The Kersleys, Murrays, and Morrises all agreed it was exceedingly pleasant, and a great advantage to meet the country people. The beautiful Miss Thorwold and her elegant friend, Mrs. Knight, told each other it was really a comfort to see a few decent carriages.

The bestowing of the military band was a blessing to the spirit of the fete. In truth, the band made a great difference. All the fiddles in Overby could not have produced so exhilarating an effect as did the wind instruments of the military ensemble. Mrs. Dermont listened to the music, watching the gay groups move with measured steps upon the sun and shadow checkered lawn. The colonel proudly inhaled the sweet air, Alfred almost forgot to think about himself, and Julia looked positively pretty.

"Inspiring!" Mrs. Stephens cried.

"Very fine indeed, ma'am," said Mr. Holingsworth.

"How divinely beautiful!" Janet Murray exclaimed.

Her sister replied, "It is like being in heaven!"

"Upon my word, my dear, this is enough to make one take a house in the country," said Mrs. Kersley, conscious they were doing exceedingly well in the world, and had as good a right to a lawn and shrubbery as some of their country neighbors. "How full of spirits Dick looks, doesn't he? And upon my honor, I think Lavinia is the handsomest girl here."

Old Mrs. Morris, the vicar's widow, looked happier than she had done for half a dozen years. Her pretty, delicate looking daughter—who she saw Ensign Wheeler offer his arm to bring her infirm mother to a bench—thought this might certainly be the happiest day of her life. Even Mrs. Verepoint, though she did not quite approve of the general style of the party, allowed that it was certainly attractive. Her twenty-year old daughter Charlotte eyed the beautiful Alfred, and determined that she must find dear Julia, who had not yet been seen.

Miss Celestina Marsh beheld the atmosphere with her whole soul, searching out her Wheeler in the crowd. She found him dutifully assisting Mrs. Morris. She looked down upon her satin shoes and thought the sweet office of rewarding him should be hers. Her feet were long and her ankles not very slender. And, while her person was in some respects rather bulky, she had both energy of character and muscle to bear her onward with a vigor that few of her acquaintances could equal. With this source of enjoyment in her heart, Miss Celestina Marsh stood next to the dainty and tranquil Charlotte Verepoint, who happened to be beside Celestina's brother, George Marsh.

Mr. Marsh politely asked Mrs. Verepoint if she would like to sit down.

"Certainly, Mr. Marsh. You shall escort me, if you please, to that bench yonder. Mrs. Morris is a great favorite with me and I shall like to sit down by her."

Celestina followed close behind him towards the Morrises. Miss Louisa Morris was dressed in the plainest white muslin frock that, by Celestina's estimation, ever a young lady wore on such an occasion. Celestina thought herself radiant in a wreath of red roses over the stiffened thin pink satin of her small bonnet. While her gown mimicked the shape of a morning dress, it concealed nothing which an evening gown could have displayed.

Louisa Morris had been given to understand there was to be dancing, and as it never occurred to her that young ladies would chose to dance in fantastical head gear, did not wear the new bonnet she had insisted her mother purchase for her. She instead trusted the beautiful headdress which nature had given her. Her silken brown curls formed into ringlets around her pretty little head, falling upon her close fitting white frock.

In approaching the bench that Mrs.Verepoint wished to occupy, the delighted Celestina took advantage of the opportunity to give Ensign Wheeler a playful tap on the shoulder with the stick of her parasol.

He turned towards her. "Good morning, Miss March. I hope I see you well?"

"I believe you have positively forgotten the way to Locklow Wood. Did I not tell you the other day in Overby, Mr. Wheeler, that my brother has the private right to fishing in the beautiful stream that runs through our estate?" Celestina turned to her brother. "George, I wish you would tell Mr. Wheeler that you do not intend to take him up as a poacher if you were to see him fishing in Locklow Meads."

George Marsh turned to address his sister and the young ensign. "I hope Mr. Wheeler knows it would give me the greatest pleasure to see him at my house, or in any part of the grounds, where he thought he could find amusement."

Mr. Wheeler accepted the extended hand of George Marsh, shook it, and moved off to address Miss Morris.

Celestina whispered in her brother's ear, "Will you let him go away then, George?"

"My dear, dearest Celestina, control your emotions. Now, come with me." George tenderly took her hand and drew it beneath his arm, leading her towards Mrs. Knight and Miss Thorwold, to whom they were slightly acquainted.

At this moment, Colonel Dermont and his lady approached the small group and welcomed them. Alfred had expressed to his parents an admiration for Miss Thorwold. Neither of them particularly admired the young lady themselves, nor had they the slightest wish to select her for a daughter-in-law, but the circumstance of their son's admiration was sufficient to place her in a position of higher consequence. Alfred had said that Miss Thorwold was the handsomest girl he had ever seen, and Miss Thorwold was therefore beyond all further question.

"Are you fond of dancing, Mr. Marsh?" the colonel asked.

"I certainly am," he replied. "May I ask the honor of waltzing with you, Miss Thorwold?"

The young lady had already smiled her acquiescence when Colonel Dermont interfered. "I beg your pardon, Mr. Marsh, but it is the purpose of Mr. Alfred Dermont to open our ball with this young lady. You will, I am sure, have the kindness to excuse my interference. And Miss Thorwold, I trust you will not refuse my son the honor of leading you out."

George Marsh felt no disappointment, for though quite aware Miss Thorwold was beautiful, he did not like her. She had an air of pretension about her. In his opinion, this was the greatest defect a young woman could have. He bowed his resignation with good grace, assuring Colonel Dermont that he would not tamper with so proper an arrangement.

Miss Thorwold, who had a fancy for Mr. Marsh of Locklow Wood, offered Colonel Dermont a smile that was bland, but beautiful. "Your son does me great honor, Colonel Dermont, and I accept with gratitude. But in the course of the morning, Mr. Marsh, I shall hope to get a tour de waltz with you."

George Marsh bowed his thanks to the group before backing out of the circle with his sister.

Celestina took the opportunity to champion her brother to her cause once more. "Go now, my dear George. Go to Mr. Wheeler and lead him off from that detestable Miss Morris. She has a mother to manage for her, and take my word for it, it is nothing in the world but the cleverness of the old woman which keeps him away from me. Go and bring him to me. And as you lead him over the lawn, be sure to fix a day for him to come early to fish at Locklow Wood. Make him understand that he is to dine with us. That is all I ask of you at this moment, George. Surely there is no great difficulty in it. Go, I tell you. I will sit down here and wait until you bring him."

# Chapter 4

Ices, coffee, and cakes were offered to every individual assembled. The band, having hushed their sounds for a few minutes, burst forth again to a waltz. Alfred Dermont looked happy and handsome, his beautiful partner all smiles and fascination.

Miss Amelia Thorwold was aware that Alfred Dermont had the greatest power of making her conspicuous by his attentions. He was, in all respects, the first young man in the company. He was the richest and most handsome, and the fete was his own. She knew it would not be possible to do better than devote herself to captivating him, so as to leave him little or no chance of ever knowing a moment of peace afterward.

Her reasoning was conclusive, and the conduct of the lovely Amelia was resigned to it. During the long hours of the fete there might have been the possibility of her relaxing during the course of it, had it not been for a trifling accident that acted effectively as a stimulant.

Julia Drummond appeared on the lawn in a fashionable and pretty white dress presented to her by the colonel for the occasion. The most elaborate toilet of her life completed, her silken black locks were parted and pushed back from her forehead, one white Camilla peeping forth from the rich knot her tresses were classically twisted into. Another of the same delicate flowers met the point in which her well fitting dress terminated in front, resting upon an innocent young bosom, as pure and nearly as white as the bloom and dress themselves.

When Alfred saw her, he looked around for his mother so he might say, "How very pretty little Julia looks!" But Mrs. Dermont was too much absorbed in wishing everyone she saw well, and he could only mutter to himself, "What a difference a dress does make!"

He looked at her repeatedly during the course of the day, a circumstance which served to keep alive Miss Thorwold's determination not to relax in the display of her fascination. She believed Julia, even with her fine eyes, raven hair, creamy skin, Camillas and all, was infinitely below her own great beauty. Nevertheless, she would not permit the attention of any man with whom she'd decided to flirt to be withdrawn from her for a single instant. Amelia made certain the innocent looking little Julia never approached them, and if it appeared she might receive a nod or smile from Alfred, Amelia instantly released a fresh rush of coquetry. Once, when the probability of this seemed particularly great, she even pressed herself upon his arm in order to render his attentions elsewhere impossible.

Her chaperone, Mrs. Knight, spent all the time Mrs. Dermont bestowed upon her to press the high fashion of Miss Thorwold's noble relations, and the remarkable esteem in which the young lady was held by the most distinguished circles in London and Paris. With all this, Mrs. Dermont became convinced that if her son wished the beautiful Amelia for his wife, there was no reason whatsoever that this wish should not be gratified.

Across the lawn, George Marsh watched the handsome young ensign his sister pined after standing close beside the blushing Louisa Morris. He looked the picture of happiness and gallantry, and George Marsh saw and understood it all. Still, he made his way to the side of Ensign Wheeler, touching the young officer on the arm.

"Will you do me the favor, Mr. Wheeler, of walking across the lawn with me to speak to my sister? She wishes that you should fix a day for coming to Locklow Wood next week, that you may get in a morning's fishing."

Ensign Wheeler, knowing perfectly well that he was only invited to this fishing for the chance of being caught himself, colored a good deal. "I should be happy to accompany you to your sister, Mr. Marsh, were I not this moment going to lead Miss

Morris to join the dancers. Pray make my compliments to Miss Marsh and explain this to her."

George Marsh made his best effort to speak gaily. "Certainly sir, but will you fix a day for giving up the pleasure of your company?"

"I am extremely sorry Mr. Marsh, but it will not be possible for me to accept your invitation. I am so constantly occupied at Overby at present that I really cannot leave the town, even for a day." He gave a stiff, though not ungraceful, bow and repossessed himself of his young partner's hand on his arm.

Had George Marsh contrived at that miserable moment to feel angry with him, it would have been a great relief. He had not a shadow of a doubt that the young ensign was acting with perfect propriety, and the part he himself played appeared to him so detestable. He felt as if he had the courage not only to tell Celestina the young ensign altogether declined her invitation, but to make her understand that it was absolutely necessary she should avoid him for the future as much as possible.

George Marsh approached his sister, who remained seated on a bench near the shrubbery, not entirely in view of the rest of the party. "Think of him no more, my dearest Celestina. His feelings towards you do not merit the return which your generous heart is ready to give. He has positively refused our invitation."

Her fierce black eyes flashed upon him. "I wish with all my soul I had given the invitation myself. I dare say you mean very well, George, but you are such a monstrous fool that it is quite impossible to trust you. What is your reason, sir, for daring to say that he does not think of me?"

"My reason, Celestina, is that he is clearly devoted to another. You are right in your suspicion that he is attached to Miss Morris. I have seen enough to convince me that this is the case."

During that very moment, it chanced that the circle of the waltz brought the charming ensign and his partner into view. The effect was instantaneous, and Celestina sunk, fainting from her seat upon the grass.

Celestina opened her eyes when her brother made no real move towards her. "Help me back to the bench, George. I feel dreadfully faint, but if you will run to the house and get me a glass of water with wine, I shall be able to get over it."

George hastened to obey her, and as he did Mrs. Dermont looked her way. Seeing the solitary Celestina Marsh with neither partner nor companion, the hostess quickened her step to inquire if the girl did not waltz.

"Oh, yes ma'am," Celestina replied. "I am particularly fond of waltzing, only I have not happened to see any dancing gentlemen with whom I am acquainted."

"Dear me! I am sorry, Miss Marsh. Do you know any of the military gentlemen? But, perhaps you would not like to dance with a stranger?"

"I should not mind at all dancing with a stranger, but I am afraid they are not likely to ask me unless they are introduced."

"Then I must take care that they are introduced. Have the kindness to excuse me for a moment, Miss Marsh."

So saying, Mrs. Dermont hastened towards a group of gentlemen, one of whom wore a red coat. With all the gentle authority of a hostess, she asked, "Will you permit me, sir, to introduce you to a partner? I have a young friend whom I wish to see dancing."

Had the question been asked by anybody but the mistress, Captain Waters would certainly have declined. He had been waiting in readiness to offer his hand for the next dance to Miss Janet Murray. As it was, to refuse was impossible, and he therefore yielded himself with the best grace he could to the lady's guidance. Quickly introduced and among the other dancers, he put his arm around the substantial waist of the delighted Celestina, and whirled her onward to her heart's content in as short a time as possible.

George Marsh reappeared with the requested water and wine, his movement halted by the apparition of Celestina, whirling rapidly on the arm of Captain Waters. Her eyes emitted sparks of rapture, and a triumphant smile displayed her large teeth.

He paused for a moment, still holding the glass in his hand, while she continued the strenuous activity until she was breathless and came to a dead stop just before him. She stood in front of her brother, retaining possession of the arm of her partner, suggesting the idea of her requiring support.

"My dearest Celestina, I hope you have not over exerted yourself."

"Good gracious, George, what nonsense you do talk! What in the world could put in your head that a waltz was likely to hurt me?"

At his quizzical look, she leaned in and whispered, "You need not look so dismal, George. It is not one man that will break my heart, I promise you."

She seized the glass from his hands and drained it to the last drop. "Thank you, George. Now, out of the way."

She handed the glass back to him. "I'm ready, Captain Waters."

Away she sprung, leaving him to meditate on the wondrous nature of women. A passing servant offered to take the glass he held, and as he raised his eyes he encountered those of Charlotte Verepoint fixed upon him. She smiled when their eyes met and in an instant George Marsh was by her side.

# Chapter 5

When the Mount family assembled at breakfast on the morning after the fete, the colonel and Mrs. Dermont were both in excellent spirits. Everything had gone off brilliantly.

"Certainly, I never did see a set of people so perfectly delighted," said Mrs. Dermont.

"What you say is quite true, my dear," replied the colonel. "I observed the same myself and must say it was all very natural, for the scene was one of great splendor and beauty. You too, Julia, seemed to enjoy it—I thought not a little. I never before saw you look so well or so gay."

Julia perked up in her seat. "Enjoy it, sir? Good gracious, how was it possible not to? It is saying very little for a girl like me to declare that I never saw anything so beautiful in my whole life.

But it is not only I who said it! Everybody—yes, I do believe everybody, kept on saying the same words!"

While his father, mother, and Julia continued to converse on all that had passed, Alfred sat at the breakfast table profoundly silent. He kept his eyes fixed upon the newspaper instead of joining in with them. He assumed the appearance of being occupied until his mother could no longer resist her desire to hear him speak on the subject.

"Set by the newspaper for one moment Alfred, and tell us whether you did not think everything went off particularly well yesterday?"

"Went off?" repeated Alfred with a tremendous sigh.

"Yes, dearest! Don't you think it was really brilliant?"

"Brilliant?"

"Why, my dearest boy, what can you be thinking of? Have you already forgotten our fete yesterday?"

"It is not very likely that I should forget it, ma'am."

"Don't plague him so," said the colonel. He was perplexed at his son's indifference to what he thought ought to interest him more than the newspaper. "It is tormenting to be talked to, my dear, when one is reading the newspaper. But I confess that our dear boy's silence does look a little as if he had not much enjoyed the party. If so, I promise you it will be the last of the kind that will be given here. Tell the truth at once Alfred, did you not enjoy it?"

"Do you honestly think sir, that I did not enjoy it? Gracious heaven, what an idea! Never did I know what it was to live until yesterday, and to pass another such day I would willingly—joyfully—consent to sacrifice half of my existence!"

His parents smiled at the admission and bobbed their heads in agreement.

Alfred stood from his chair. "Come Julia. I must speak to you."

Julia jumped from her own chair and, Alfred leading the way, they entered his own quiet little study.

"Shut the door, Julia."

Once the door was shut, Julia took a seat. She feared her heart was beating almost audibly.

"Oh, Julia!" he began. "We have read together of the power of love, but until yesterday—Julia! I am ten thousand fathom deep in love!"

Julia's heart nearly leapt from her chest. If her thoughts could be articulated, she might have said, *It is come then!*

"Ten million thousand fathom deep in love with the angelic Amelia Thorwold!"

The effect Alfred's declaration had on Julia felt to her like a large bucket of cold water upon a red hot iron. Alfred's words converted in her something that was glowing and bright, to a state completely the reverse—but it also rendered strong and firm, that which the instant before, had been soft and yielding. They say that the last moments of consciousness in a wretch that is drowning is the passing of every event that has happened in their lives, a life one is about to quit. In like manner did Julia Drummond, in one rapid glance, review the whole course of weakness and presumption to which she had been guilty in her estimation of Alfred.

She knew far better than anyone else in the world the superiority of Alfred to all others around them. That she, for a single instant, had thought he could dream of partnering himself with her—it was preposterous. "But if not enough, it is all I can offer," Julia thought, her heart swelling with intensity and resolution. "I will firmly adhere myself to my purpose, and live as his friend, not falling again on the madness which seized me today."

Julia looked steadfastly in the face of her friend, taking her first lesson in endurance from his playful glance.

"Why Julia, you are absolutely good for nothing by way of a confidante and comforter! I made you come with me here because I thought I should like better for you to tell my father and mother that I intend to propose to Miss Thorwold immediately, than have the—the sort of awkwardness of doing it myself. But you look as if you are frightened out of your wits, and I'm sure if you go to them they will take fright themselves at once!"

Julia attempted a smile in reply, but what she presented only made her look more strange and unlike herself.

"What in the world is the matter with you, Julia? Surely you have not taken into your silly little head that Amelia is not a proper match for me? As to her fortune, I know nothing of it, and you may tell my father and mother that I don't care a single straw whether or not she has a hundred thousand pounds or a sixpence. As to family, we all know she is highly connected. On personal merit, where shall I ever find any human being equal to her? Tell me, Julia, and be sure you say exactly what you think—have you ever seen anything as heavenly beautiful as Amelia Thorwold?"

Julia snapped back to her senses. "She is beautiful indeed, Alfred. Tell me exactly what you wish me to say to my guardian and Mrs. Dermont, and depend upon it I will say it without forgetting a word."

"How can you be such a fool, Julia? I am much too agitated to know exactly what to say. You now know the state of my case, my dear, and I want you to tell them that I have made you my confidante, and opened my heart to you. You may tell them it is quite clear that no power on earth will ever induce me to marry anyone else. Tell them she is an angel, and that you wish them joy in having such a daughter. If all this passes between you and them, all the worst part of the business will be over before I come upon the scene. And then, dear souls, they will only have to kiss me and wish me joy. Go then, my darling girl, go at once! Then come back here when you think the proper time is come for me to make my appearance."

"I will not delay for an instant."

In a moment the door of the room was closed between them.

Julia stood before the entrance of the breakfast room to recover her breath, and to assure herself she was physically capable of performing the task before her. Of her own courage and power to conceal the feelings which had become the first duty of her life to conquer, she had no misgivings. She had once in her life, about a year before, fainted. It was the consequence of sudden terror, on hearing Alfred's gun discharge and thinking he might have discharged it on himself. She was worried of fainting again the moment she was to disclose the news of which she was the messenger.

She took a deep breath and entered the breakfast room, where she found the colonel and his lady in a state of vehement curiosity to know why their son had left their presence so abruptly. They sat perfectly still, not even having taken the liberty of ringing to have the breakfast things removed.

"I have got something very particular, very unexpected to tell you. You must please both of you listen to me kindly, as indeed, you always do."

She stopped for a moment in order to figure out the words she could best use to convey that Alfred was in love.

Mrs. Dermont's color heightened in her cheeks. "Listen kindly? That must depend a good deal on the sort of thing you have got to say, Miss Drummond."

Had Julia been quite composed, the strangeness of Mrs. Dermont's appellation would doubtless have struck her. As it was, she took no notice. "Alfred wants you to know at once, but without telling you himself, that he is very much in love."

The colonel burst into a joyous laugh, rubbing his hands together in glee. "God bless his dear heart! Is he indeed? So much the better, Julia, so much the better! A young man in his station in life, and with such prospects, ought not enter his twenty first year without having some such idea as that come into his head. I am glad to hear it, my dear. I am, upon my soul, and so you may tell him!"

"Upon my word, colonel, I think that must depend a good deal upon who it is he fancies himself in love with," said Mrs. Dermont. "Alfred may have taken it into his young head to like someone today whom he would be very much ashamed to be marrying tomorrow."

These words brought such an accession of color to the cheeks of poor Julia that Mrs. Dermont, whose eyes were fixed upon her, no longer felt the least doubt that she was the heroin of her own tale. She rose impatiently from her chair and, pushing Julia aside, walked towards the door.

Julia sprung toward her and seized her hand. "Please stay, Mrs. Dermont! You have not heard more than half my message yet! I have not told you who the lady is! Pray do not leave until I have told you that!"

Mrs. Dermont stopped short in her hurried progress to the door. "Speak out at once, Julia. Who is the lady?"

"Miss Thorwold," Julia replied distinctly.

"Miss Thorwold!" exclaimed the colonel.

"Miss Thorwold?" cried Mrs. Dermont.

Though he spoke in admiration and she spoke interrogatively, there was nothing in either voice which sounded at all like displeasure.

"The boy shows good taste," said the colonel. "Nobody can deny that. She is a lovely creature."

"He has made a choice not only of the handsomest, but of the most highly connected and distinguished young lady that he could have found," added Mrs. Dermont.

"As far as I am concerned, my dear, I shall make no objection," the colonel said. "Young men in the position of Alfred ought to marry early. He is heir to a property that justifies in him what might be considered imprudent in others. Tell him to come to us, my dear girl. And tell him he has nothing to fear. I would go to him myself, only I think it might have the air of breaking in upon his privacy."

"And tell him also that he shall find his adoring mother, as he has ever found her, devoted to his happiness."

She found Alfred pacing up and down the hall, and shared the news with him.

"Thank heaven that's over! And thank you too, dear Julia. You have been very kind to me!"

They parted, Alfred to receive his parents tenderest assurances of his choice, and Julia to the longed for solitude of her own apartment. She almost smiled now at the wild folly which could have made her dream, even for an instant, that such a being as Alfred could select *her* for his wife. She told herself with patient resignation that different sorts of people had different sorts of happiness assigned to them. Those who were hopelessly unhappy and stubbornly resisted the arrangements of Providence, setting their wishes upon some impossible fancy, would probably not prove productive of real happiness if ever obtained by the wisher.

After a few hours of seclusion in her room, Julia felt in no danger of having her youth blasted by unhappy love. On the contrary, she looked forward to immense happiness from watching the happiness of her friend Alfred, his beautiful wife, and their dear children. Oh, how she should love those children!

# Chapter 6

"I will write to Mrs. Knight instantly," Mrs. Dermont said. "I shall ask her to come and dine here any day that you fix, my dearest Alfred."

Alfred struck his forehead with his hand. "Ask her to dine here, ma'am? Is that all you mean to do? Do you suppose that I can propose to her as I take off her shawl when she arrives, or when I put it on at her departure?"

The colonel put his hand up in his wife's defense. "No, no, Alfred! Your mother does not mean any such nonsense, I am sure. When they come to dinner, they must, of course, stay the three days that our company generally do. Of course, my dear boy, your mother intended nothing else."

"You really must give me time, and whether I confess my feelings at the end of three days or thirty, I should wish that Miss Thorwold should be invited to stay here for a month."

"Most certainly she shall, Alfred. For exactly as long as you like," his mother replied eagerly.

Mrs. Dermont fixed her eyes on the colonel's face, looking a little embarrassed. "Although, I hardly know either of the ladies at all. How can we find an excuse for asking her for so long a time? It will seem rather odd and familiar to her, will it not, my dear? Especially considering before the fete she never was at our house at all."

Alfred clasped his hands and looked the picture of misery. "Is that the way to talk to a man so distractedly in love? Odd? Familiar? What words are these when my life is at stake?"

Mrs. Dermont was inexpressibly distressed. "My dear, dear boy! There is nothing in the whole world which I would not do to make you happy. If I am frightened of doing anything out of the common way, it is only because I dread the idea of her thinking us less acquainted with the manners of people of fashion. You should remember, my dear, how very highly connected Miss Thorwold is, and that for this reason and no other, we ought to be careful that everything we do is in the proper style. What do you think about it, colonel?"

"I admit that I do not at this moment see my way very clearly. We must think on it a little. Perhaps our dear Alfred himself may suggest something?"

"Yes, I will suggest something. I will suggest, if you please, that you should send for Julia this instant. She knows the state of my affections and she is such a quick witted little creature. I have no doubt she will invent some scheme or other that will make the matter easy. I will go and look for her myself."

Alfred had no difficulty finding her. She had just left her room with a bonnet on her head and a parasol in her hand. She was going out to enjoy a solitary walk in the shrubberies.

"Do not go out just yet, Julia." Alfred took the parasol from her hand. "We want you very much in the breakfast room. My father and mother are all kindness, but they are puzzling their poor, dear heads about matters I dare say you will find easy enough to make smooth. And don't be afraid to dictate, as you call it sometimes, because it is exactly what the dear souls are longing for."

They moved swiftly to the breakfast room and Alfred presented Julia to the council, not having given her any intimation of the subject upon which she was to be consulted.

Mrs. Dermont said in her most pleasant tone, "Come here, Julia, and sit down by me. Let us hear what sort of invention your young head can hit upon. Of course you have told her, Alfred, where the difficulty lies?"

"No indeed, I have left that to you, for I don't understand the difficulty. I should not wonder much if Julia did not, either."

Mrs. Dermont, still in good humor, said, "Oh dear me! When young men fall in love they can see nothing! But this is the difficulty, Julia. Alfred is anxious to have Miss Thorwold invited to stay here for a good, long visit—a month, perhaps. Or something of that sort. Now the question is, how are we to find any reason for inviting her, which we may assign, to both herself and Mrs. Knight, without alluding to the real reason? For dear Alfred will not have a word said about that at present. He chooses to take the breaking it to her entirely upon himself, and to select his own time for it. What can we invent now to say to her?"

Julia listened to every word of this with earnest attention and without the least bit of agitation or discomposure. For the space of about two minutes she remained silent, then smiled. "I think there is a way in which you might do it without any awkwardness at all, if it will not be giving you too much trouble."

"Trouble, child? How can you possibly suppose that I should care for trouble at such a moment as this? Go on, let us hear what you have to say, whether there is sense in it or not."

Julia smiled again, looking almost as pretty as she had done the day before. "Well then, I suggest Mrs. Dermont should drive over tomorrow to Mrs. Knight and tell her that the young people all seemed to enjoy the fete so much, particularly the dining in the tent, that the colonel has requested the officers allow the tents to remain on ground while the fine weather lasts. Tell her you intend to have a few of your young neighbors to pass a little time at the Mount, and that they might amuse themselves with archery, dancing, or anything they liked. If Miss Thorwold would be one of the party, it would give you great pleasure."

Alfred clapped his hands and looked to Julia. "Capital idea!"

Mrs. Dermont laughed. "Well done, Julia! Has she not hit upon a good scheme, colonel?"

"As far as I may presume to judge on such matters, I must say that I think this plan of Julia's is admirable. It not only clears any objections with Mrs. Knight, but with a few more young people staying, nobody can suspect she is invited here for the purpose of giving Alfred an opportunity to know her better and propose."

"I could not help thinking the other day how you are getting to look quite the young woman, Julia," Mrs. Dermont offered. "We must now treat you as one. Come, tell me, who shall we invite?"

"If Alfred thinks two or three couples will be enough, that is what I would suggest," Julia replied.

"Perfectly adequate, Julia. I shall care very little how many other couples there are."

"Then, along with Miss Thorwold, would not Miss Verepoint and Miss Marsh be young ladies enough?"

"Yes, yes," Alfred answered."George Marsh is one of the few men whom I should like to have staying in the house. As for his sister, we all know she will go on spinning from night to morning if you let her."

"But who shall we have dance with her, Alfred?" Mrs. Dermont asked. "I do not think I should like to have her here that long if we could not manage to get a partner for her."

Alfred thought for a moment. "Then you must ask Mr. and Mrs. Stephens. You saw what a waltzer he was—very nearly as good as Marsh, himself."

"I heard Mrs. Stephens say that they were going to paint their dining room," Julia said. "Might you ask them on that account, to get them away from the dreaded smell of paint?"

"You are an angel, Julia!" Alfred exclaimed. "There ma'am, now I am sure every possible objection is answered. There can be no reason for asking old Mrs. Verepoint, as Charlotte has stayed here by herself before now. That room may then be offered to Mrs. Knight. And dear Julia can take a dance now and then if she likes it, anytime my divine Amelia gets tired. I would take a turn with you myself, Julia. That is, provided I do not have anything particular to say to her while she is sitting down."

"It is settled then!" Mrs. Dermont said excitedly.

Alfred's handsome face brightened even further into an expression of extreme delight. "You are all three the very dearest and best people that were ever born. It is no good for me to attempt telling any of you how grateful I feel, for unless you were as much in love as I am it is impossible you could understand me. As to you, Julia, I hope someday or other you will be in love yourself. When the time comes, you shall see if I am not grateful! I will move heaven and earth, my dear, to arrange things for you as nicely as you have now done for me."

# Chapter 7

Fortunately, no difficulties of any kind arose to impede the execution of the plan they had fixed upon. Mrs. Knight and Miss Thorwold both bowed and smiled at the invitation, saying that they were sure it would make them very happy. Mrs. Dermont waited for nothing more and took rather a hurried leave, saying she had one or two more calls to make. Having happily achieved the principle part of her commission, she was determined not to return home until she had arranged the whole party in the manner proposed.

Charlotte Verepoint colored a good deal when told who would be present and for about half a moment considered declining. In her opinion, the person, dress, voice, and manner of Celestina Marsh, as she had seen at the fete, were all disagreeable to her. However, before she felt quite ready to speak for herself, her mother had spoken for her and agreed she would join for at least a few days. After this it was quite impossible for Charlotte to invent any objection. So onward went the happy Mrs. Dermont, with as little loss of time as possible.

Beech Hill was her next stop where she found the Stephens' at home. She was at first a little dismayed by the sight of their American friend, Mr. Holingsworth, whom the whole of the Mount family had forgotten.

"It won't do," thought Mrs. Dermont. "I must go away without saying anything about it."

As fate would have it, the very moment she began trying to construct how best to account for her oddly timed visit, a servant entered and inquired whether he'd like his baggage taken to the inn—where the London coach was to stop for him. With his plan for departure decidedly fixed, Mrs. Dermont skillfully led the conversation to the subject of paint and its injurious effects on the constitution. In a most amiable manner, she offered a few days respite at the Mount. Mr. and Mrs. Stephens could then have their decorators go on with their work without any ill effects on their persons produced by it.

Mrs. Stephens colored with pleasure at this flattering proof of attention from the so decidedly first family of the neighborhood. She accepted, even without the ceremony of first consulting her husband. Mr. Stephens assured Mrs. Dermont that her invitation was, on every account, the most agreeable one he could have received.

"Well now, I am out of luck, I expect," said Mr. Holingsworth. "I suppose they wouldn't give me back my money at the coach office, would they?"

Without answering, Mrs. Dermont politely made her excuses for leaving them abruptly, and moved with rather a more rapid step than usual towards her carriage. She set off to Locklow Wood, her drive altogether rather a long one for her stately coach horses. As she approached the house, she saw Mr. Marsh on the gravel road that led to it. He removed his hat as she passed in the carriage and hastened forward to hand her from her carriage. His surprise that the lady of the Mount should visit was evident. Mrs. Dermont explained the object of her visit, which he seemed to welcome with great satisfaction.

"Is your sister at home, Mr. Marsh?"

His answer was in the affirmative.

"Then perhaps you would have the kindness to inform her of the purpose of my visit, and bring me her answer without my leaving the carriage? For it is so late that I shall hardly have time to get home before the dressing bell rings."

"She will, I am sure, come to the carriage to speak to you in a moment," he replied.

Mr. Marsh made his way to the house. Mrs. Dermont settled back in her seat thinking what a shame it was that Mr. and Miss Marsh should be alone at Locklow Wood, their parents both deceased. For some time she was so pleasantly occupied recalling the success of all her invitations, that she sat waiting with no feeling of impatience. The restless pawing of her horses reminded her she had been sitting there for an immense time, and that it was quite impossible she could stay there all day. She called to the footman to ring the house bell and inquire whether she could have the pleasure of seeing Miss Marsh.

The man obeyed and a maid servant answered, disappearing inside with the message. She returned again almost immediately with the assurance that Miss Marsh was making the greatest of haste, and would be there in no time.

Again, Mrs. Dermont had recourse to her thoughts, arguing with herself as to whether or not she should drive a half-mile out of her way to the butcher. She would tell him to come out immediately to receive orders for the unexpected demands about to be made on his stock and trade.

Still, Miss Marsh failed to appear, and again the patience of Mrs. Dermont began to wear thin. She told her footman to ring the bell once more, adding that if the young lady was engaged, Mrs. Dermont would beg her to have the kindness to send her answer through the maid.

The maid was delivered the message again and vanished behind the door. Instead of returning, the striking figure of Celestina herself now appeared. She approached with hurried steps and her head bent low, trying to protect the limp ringlets she had been so carefully arranging from the summer breeze. Mrs. Dermont met her eyes with a grave air, apologized for having been obliged to hurry her, then repeated—with considerable stateliness—the invitation she said she presumed had already been delivered to her. Celestina, with her red cheeks and lank ringlets, flashed her inconceivably broad grin and accepted the blessing offered.

From Locklow Wood, Mrs. Dermont proceeded to the butcher's shop. Her guests all confirmed, she went about the task of demanding a monopoly on his sweetbreads, sirloins, fillets of veal, and fore-quarters of lamb. The butcher promised not only to do all he could, but to employ assistance should his own resources fail.

Mrs. Dermont drove up to her own door, a little late and a good deal fatigued, but happy beyond measure of having done her duty.

She felt, and with reason, that she should be proud to meet both Alfred and her housekeeper. She felt that they must both of them approve and admire her. She was not disappointed by the reception she received from either.

Alfred met her in the hall and seized upon her hand. "Well mother?"

"Well, Alfred!" she replied. "They are to come, all of them!"

"All, my dearest mother? How can you have contrived to see them all?"

"There is nothing like an earnest good will, my darling son, to enable one to get through business quickly. I have not only seen all the guests, but have seen the butcher as well. I hope taking such measures will insure the party against all risk of starvation."

"You are the very best and dearest mother that ever a son had!"

"We shall have them the next day but one after tomorrow. I could not have them before, my dear, because there are so many rooms to make ready. Six rooms, Alfred, besides the ladies' maids. We shall be quite full and will have no room for that Miss Celestina, save for one of those we would use for a bachelor. I hope the Marsh blood will not be affronted."

"The bachelors' rooms are excellent mother, fit for any lady," Alfred replied. "But where is Miss Thorwold to sleep, mother?"

"In the pink room, Alfred. It is the gayest looking, and I think it likely Miss Thorwold will prefer it to the damask room—though that is the handsomest, to be sure. I shall put Mrs. Knight in the damask room, and they will be close together, only a dressing room between. You think she would like the pink room best, don't you Alfred?"

"It is exactly the one I would have chosen for her! *Couleur de rose!* Yes, it is exactly the room for her."

Mrs. Dermont mounted the stairs to her dressing room to quickly dress for dinner, which was already waiting. As she disappeared, Julia emerged, and Alfred was by the side of his confidante almost instantly. "She is coming, Julia! Everything has been done according to your plan. Mother has seen them all, and they are all to come the next day but one after tomorrow! Is the pianoforte in good tune, Julia? I hope, my dearest Julia, that you will enjoy it!"

Julia finished sliding her hand into a glove, having just readied herself for dinner. "I am very glad!"

Alfred bound down the stairs, Julia making her decent in the manner proper for a young lady. She was sincerely glad for him, saying to herself, "This will be the time for me to get acquainted with Miss Thorwold. I will be so very kind, so very attentive, so very devoted to her! If I were she, I don't suppose I should see or hear anything but Alfred."

# Chapter 8

Never had any lady more cause to rejoice in a well ordered household, than had Mrs. Dermont on the present occasion. Considerably before the hour at which the first of the expected guests arrived, not only was the whole house in the most perfect order, but the flower beds looked as if they were dressed for company. Not a trace of the fete was left upon the well swept, well watered, and well rolled lawn except the lovely marquees. The whole company arrived with great propriety, so as to give themselves exactly enough time to dress for dinner. They assembled in the drawing room at seven o'clock.

The colonel walked to a window and addressed the whole circle of guests. "What a beautiful afternoon it is. We must not sit long at the table today as if we were a formal dinner party. The fair ladies must all wrap themselves up in their shawls and let us enjoy a stroll in the grounds before tea."

Alfred looked at him with an expression that spoke a volume of gratitude and love, then addressed the beautiful Amelia. "My father's proposal is not a bad one, Miss Thorwold. Is it not a misery on such a day as today, to be kept in a dining room?"

He ventured to put his hand upon the back of her chair, a chair which he stood behind. She turned half around and gazed upwards towards him. "Oh yes, Mr. Dermont. Don't you delight in the country?"

Alfred, whose only two visits to London had been short and far between, hesitated for an instant. He replied in a low voice, "Upon my honor, Miss Thorwold, I can easily believe it possible, that in some situations, a man may lose all consciousness of the nature of the place he stands. He may take trees for palaces and a crowded street for a wooded forest. A human voice may sound to him sweeter than a symphonic flute. And he may mistake—oh, how easily!—a woman for an angel."

Miss Thorwold smiled. "What an enthusiast you are!"

As Alfred stood entranced by Miss Thorwold's smile, the door was opened and dinner was announced.

The scarcity of gentlemen on the present occasion left little to be done by way of pairs, and settled itself, almost by necessity. The colonel, of course, gave his arm to Mrs. Knight, Mrs. Dermont yielded hers to Mr Stephens, and the graceful Alfred offered his arm to Miss Thorwold. George Marsh stood for a moment, confused as to whether he should escort the married Mrs.

Stephens, or Miss Verepoint, the heiress to a manor of Stoke and the acres attached to it. His long descended, old fashioned prejudice of class made him deem it his duty to take charge of the spinster Miss instead of the married lady. Had Mrs. Dermont not already entered the dining room, she would have been greatly shocked to see a married lady pass from the drawing room without a gentleman to escort her. Alfred had refused to invite an officer that might have made their numbers even, but Julia saved them all from embarrassment with a quick plot.

"Miss Marsh, I think you must give your arm to Mrs. Stephens. It is so difficult to get an equal number of gentlemen and ladies!"

Julia followed in last and entered the dining room unnoticed, seated at the colonel's left hand, nobody knew how.

Nothing particular by way of conversation took place during the dinner. Mrs. Knight and Colonel Dermont spoke of nothing that bore any significance. Mrs. Dermont and Mr. Stephens talked more, because the gentleman had a good deal he liked to say. He mostly discussed what he had done or was going to do at Beech Hill. Mrs. Dermont smiled from time to time obligingly and replied accordingly.

Mrs. Stephens talked a good deal to Miss Marsh, considering she was but a woman. It occurred to Mrs. Stephens that it might prove agreeable to befriend Celestina. In her situation it was fashionable to have a single young lady as a companion, one that might be able to come stay with her a few days at a time. She thought Miss Marsh quite plain, which removed the only objection to this sort of domestic intimacy in a married household. With a sincere effort on Mrs. Stephens' part, by the end of the dinner, it could be said they had gotten on wonderfully. They recommended several dishes to each other and, quite affectionately, had gone the length of saying they hoped to become very good neighbors.

The conversations were quiet and intimate between Miss Verepoint and Mr. Marsh, and Miss Thorwold and Mr. Alfred Dermont. None spoke hardly above a whisper, their heads inclined towards their dinner companions in undisturbed dialogue. Julia did not utter a syllable from the time she entered the room to that of her quitting it. The rest of the company were so completely divided into cozy pairs, her doing otherwise was nearly impossible.

When dinner concluded and Mrs. Dermont rose, Alfred flew to the door so that he might open it for the ladies to pass. He stopped his mother and begged her earnestly to let them have coffee on the lawn—and not be very long before she sent to let them know that it was ready.

"It shall be all right, dearest," she whispered. "The tent, I suppose?"

Alfred nodded his head in approval and, after an earnest glance at the retreating figure of Amelia, suffered his mother to pass.

He proceeded with the men into the smoking room, paying little attention to his cards, waiting for the moment they might make a move towards the lawn.

The coffee was taken under the shelter of Major Sommerton's marquee by both those who enjoyed the *al fresco* style, and those who did not. The moon shone full upon them before they had done with it. Mrs. Knight confessed she thought it cold, and Mrs. Stephens declared that she dare not venture to run any risks. Miss Verepoint, taking the arm of Julia, walked decidedly towards the house, while Mr. Marsh followed at a respectful distance. Mr. Stephens yielded himself to the colonel and listened to all he had to say about two or three of his principal farmers.

Alfred saw all this and decided, after managing everything so beautifully, he would not be cheated out of a walk in the shrubberies with Miss Thorwold.

He went to the side of his mother and took her arm. "You will not go in, ma'am. Take the arm of Miss Marsh and ask her to walk with you to the shrubbery. There is not a moment to be lost! They are both going towards the house, but this is exactly the moment I really cared for!"

Mrs. Dermont's particular dislike of Miss Celestina could not avail to prevent her from stepping forward and performing what Alfred asked. With a movement most unusually quick, she startled the young lady by abruptly taking hold of her arm and saying, "Indeed, I cannot let you go in, my dears, until I have shown you how pretty our oak tree glades look by moonlight!"

# Chapter 9

"I have sent away the maid, Amelia. I suppose you do not want her?"

These words, though softly pronounced, startled the beautiful Amelia Thorwold. She stood yawning before her mirror, the first evening of her visit at the Mount at a close.

"Good heaven, Mrs. Knight! How you startled me! No, certainly I do not much want a maid tonight. I am so horridly tired, that if I had fifty maids, I would not have my hair brushed now. But what is the matter? Why did you send her to bed?"

Mrs. Knight stretched her weary person on a chaise lounge at no great distance from her friend. "The matter, dear Amelia, is that I wish to have a conversation with you before we go to sleep. We both agreed to come here, I believe, with the same motive—to give this blooming young squire time and opportunity to fall in love with you. At least, I can answer for myself, that I hate staying in a dull country house, among a set of people who have not a single idea in common with me. Am I right in supposing it was your motive also? I do beg and entreat you to tell me the truth."

Miss Thorwold yawned. "Yes. If I know my own heart, as the heroines say, it certainly was my motive."

"Amelia! I will have no jesting! Please forgive me, but I must remind you that you are not in a position to permit any sort of levity on such a subject. Is it your intention to marry this young Dermont, if you can?"

Miss Thorwold looked into the glass before which she had seated herself. "Do you really feel any doubt as to the purpose of the Dermont's giving us this most singular invitation?"

"No, certainly not. It does not require much acuteness to read the whole story from first to last. This youth, the hope, the only hope of his snugly well acred family, has doubtless been the petted idol of both mother and father. It is not very difficult to see this has ended in him having his own way in everything. Your charms, my dear, are quite the kind to inflame the heart of such a youth. He has never yet passed a season in town and is quite unconscious of the fact that there are many Amelias to be had. Now, as I guess, this unsophisticated youth made up his mind to believe that no second goddess of equal perfection can walk the earth. He has informed mama and papa that he cannot, by any means, think of living without marrying Miss Thorwold. To be sure, the set they have got together does not promise much in the way of social enjoyment during our stay in this pretty village of

Stoke. You might be able to find ways and means, my dear, of varying the scene a little. Be this as it may, you have no reason to quarrel with me for doubting the reality of your conquest, and this is not on account of your previous disappointments. I know perfectly well the total difference in characters and scene may be safely calculated upon as likely to lead to a different catastrophe. I am afraid for you, Amelia. I am dreadfully afraid that when you get heartily sick of this place and the people, including young Dermont himself—who, handsome as he is, will soon become a horrible bore with his total ignorance—that you will begin to sneer when you ought to smile. You will yawn when you ought to sigh. It is my duty for Lord Ripley's sake, who really, has enough to plague him already, to tell you I must insist you take care what you are about. Do not expose me to this detestable bore for nothing."

Amelia began removing the rings from her slender fingers with a sullen expression.

"I really wish, Mrs. Knight, that when you think proper to lecture me, you would do so in your own name, and not my uncles. Nor is it at all necessary that you should so often endeavor to impress upon my mind, that whatever interest you have in me, is only because I belong to him. Were I you, I really should not be so anxious to point this out. I only say this to show that, notwithstanding your having half a dozen more years experience than myself, I am not quite incapable of giving advice in my turn. Do not let us quarrel. It would be exceedingly silly for many reasons. You are lively and agreeable, and your house is a great convenience to me. I am, I presume, rather ornamental. My presence is occasionally very convenient to you. So pray let us continue to be the same affectionate friends as usual. As to all you have said, my dear, concerning Master Alfred Dermont and his expected thousands per annum, I have nothing whatsoever against it. Yes, he is an only son and heir. I have no doubt were I mistress of this place I could make it look decently respectable. Neither will I deny that you have some reason to be afraid for me, seeing that I am a good deal afraid for myself. If it could be done at once, Mrs. Knight, if I could be married to the boy before breakfast tomorrow morning, I think it certain he would find the cash to discharge my various little bills. Various bills I was absolutely obliged to run up when my mother died. I think this consideration would inspire me with strength to marry him in the morning. But whether my poor, shattered spirits would bear the wear and tear of his young love—backed by all the delicate attentions of his parents—from noon until dewy eve, through heaven knows how many days…I cannot tell."

"Until dewy eve, my dear," said a laughing Mrs. Knight. "Pray do not have the belief you shall escape the arrival of dewy eve. It seems likely you will have to keep company with dewy eve herself in all her dripping freshness. Did you not look at that girl who sat to the left of the colonel tonight? She cannot be much older than sixteen. You are nine and twenty. I admit you do not look a day older than three and twenty, and the young Dermont who has not done a single season in town does not know how many you have done yourself. Fortunately, you have a way of getting up a head, and face too, for a night's wear, in a style that would defy anything. But, for the sake of your silk dresses and shoes, I would yield immediately to his wooing, Amelia. It is really too dangerous."

"I am exceedingly grateful for your kind attention to me and my suitor, Mrs. Knight. As neither dress nor shoes are paid for, that cost will fall on upon the person who is amused, and not on the one who causes amusement. But all jesting aside, the real question is, must I marry this boy at all? Is there no other way to escape? What is the worst that can happen if I say I won't?"

"My dear, rather ask yourself what is the best that can happen to you? You know as well as I do, that since you first came out—and made such an immense sensation at Almack's—since that time you have been disappointed by at least a dozen men of rank and fortune. They have all appeared to be passionately in love with you, but they all slunk off without making any direct proposal. Ask yourself, what is the very best you can expect if you let this chance escape? In a very few months, beautiful as you are, you will be thirty. You will be deeply in debt, without a shilling in the world, and the only near relation you have is exceedingly out of humor with you. You have not justified your uncle's brilliant hope of your making a good match and I don't believe, having failed by the age of thirty, he would ever take notice of you again. What is there in this young man that you can possibly object to seriously? He is decidedly one of the most handsome lads that ever was seen, and really, very far from being awkward or stupid. I will not scruple to declare that you refusing him under all the circumstances would be an act of outrageous folly. I should not think I was doing my duty, as a friend of Lord Ripley, if I did not tell you beforehand, that I could never take notice of you afterward. As I say, Amelia, this game you play is dangerous and you will, as you always do, slip up. Do not drag it out so he might find fault in you and change his mind before he even makes an offer. I must insist upon you letting me know what your intentions are. Will you be so obliging as to answer me?"

Miss Thorwold turned her head so her *friend* would escape seeing the look of scorn she was unable to suppress. She quickly recomposed herself and returned to Mrs. Knight. "Considering your great observations, my dear friend, it is rather extraordinary you should doubt my intentions of accepting this enamored boy. I would only consider refusal if I happened to have some slight ground of hope that I might marry someone I liked better. Do tell me, will you, how should you like to marry a pretty boy who is duller than a fat weed? How should you like to marry a juvenile innocent, particularly one so much in love as to not leave a glimpse of hope that he would ever let you remain in peace, while he amused himself elsewhere? How would you like it, my charming friend?"

Mrs. Knight knit her handsome brows. "I am half a dozen years older than you are, you know. You keep this in your head so constantly on most occasions, that it is hardly fair you should forget it on this one. But let us leave wit, Amelia, and return to wisdom. It is too late in the day for you to risk losing a good establishment for any slight hope of someone you might like better. I confess, my dear Miss Thorwold, I am not aware of what direction any such hope can lie. I will not do you the great injustice to believe for a single instant that any thought of Lord William Hammond can still hold a place in your memory."

"On the contrary, my dear madam, you will be doing me a great injustice if you doubt it," returned Miss Thorwold. "Circumstances over which I have no control render it exceedingly desirable that I marry someone or other without any further loss of time. It is within the reach of probability that I shall be arrested if I do not. You see, my dear lady, you cannot put this in a plainer light that I put it myself. Nevertheless, I, who must know better than anybody else what has passed between Lord William and myself, I am decidedly of the opinion there is more than hope. There is very near certainty of his coming forward again, if he could hear of this new lover."

"A very desperate game to play, I promise you. Here, on this grassy Mount, stands a young man as free from any species of vice as the angelic denizens of heaven. He is beautiful, he is innocent, and you have him in your grasp. You gamble, my dear. You gamble recklessly."

"He is innocent and nearly ten years my junior, Mrs. Knight. Lord William is a more than ten years my senior. Lord William Hammond, the darling of Almack's, the pride of the park, the glory of the drawing room, the pet of the boudoir, and the sovereign of the opera. Whereas Mr. Alfred Dermont is the darling of his mama, the pride of the Mount, the glory of its drawing room, the pet of all the young ladies that come to it, and the sovereign of the illustrious village of Stoke. I do feel the tremendous truth of every word you have uttered on the necessity of my quickly marrying. I am ready to give you my most solemn promise to be guided solely by your advice, provided you will give me one more chance with Lord William."

"Provided *I* give you another chance, Amelia? What on earth have I got to do with it? You do not mean that I am to take you back to London at this time of year?"

"Certainly not, my dear friend," Amelia replied. "Only invite Lord William to Crosby for a day or two. You have only to follow the bright example of these fine people and give a fete. That makes inviting him the most natural thing in the world. Only yesterday, you said you must do something, and yours may be an archery party, if you like."

"I wonder whether it would be possible to get your uncle out of town for a day or two?"

"Most certainly you could, for the sake of an archery meeting. Coming to see me would be such a beautiful excuse to give Lady Ripley, who, according to somewhere or other, is getting worse by the minute and not expected to live. How delightful it would be if I were to have *you* for an aunt, after all!"

Mrs. Knight knew it was ugly, but it still made her wonder. She replied, "If I were to consent to this, Amelia, how should you behave to this young Dermont in the interval?"

"In a manner I will venture to say should satisfy you," Miss Thorwold returned.

"Well then, I will now release you. Good night, my dear." said Mrs. Knight, rising and kissing her forehead. "I will meditate on your proposal before I decide. If I think I can get a sufficient number of people together, it is likely enough that I may accede to it. For, in truth, I hate to vex you, Amelia!"

# Chapter 10

Alfred stood ready at the door of the breakfast room with a bouquet of the choicest flowers from the green house, which was received by Miss Thorwold with a sincere smile.

The rest of the party were seated, which made his leading her to a pair of unoccupied chairs an act that caused most of the company to exchange looks. The delicate bloom upon the cheeks of Miss Thorwold was unchanged by the attention, whereas Alfred became very red, and Julia went pale.

Mrs. Stephens fixed her eyes on the splendid bouquet. "What lovely flowers! I have not seen such flowers this year, and must beg someone will have pity and compassion on my desire for a few."

Celestina, determined to secure a friendship with the lady and an invitation to stay, turned to Mrs. Stephens with all the charming vivacity she could muster. "I wish you might appoint me to be your flower gatherer. Do you know, there is nothing I delight in so much as devoting myself to young married women! I always think they are so interesting and so very agreeable."

Mrs. Stephens and Celestina began to make their plan for the morning.

Alfred leaned in towards Miss Thorwold and declared in a low voice, "I'm afraid that we must not venture to think of groves and gardens during the early hours of the day. There are faces which should not only be guarded from the winds of heaven, but even from its sunny smiles. We never think that the tint upon a peach might grow too ruddy, but there are cheeks which, in their tender ripeness, even the slightest change might cause every looker-on to put on mourning."

"Are there?" replied Miss Thorwold. She turned her head towards him and allowed her eyes to rest upon Alfred's. "But do you not think," she added in a low voice, "that there are moods and moments which are apt to make everybody forget everything?"

"Do I?" he returned in the lowest of all whispers. "Do I?"

No words which could have possibly been spoken by either would have equaled in eloquence the silence that followed. When this had lasted just long enough, Amelia said, "I believe you have some very pretty woodland scenery in this neighborhood, have you not?"

Alfred released a sigh. "I have thought so, until I began to suspect that such beauty could only belong to one object in nature. Such scenery, however, you might safely venture to look at if you would not fear to trust yourself to my driving. My mother has the safest little carriage with a pair of ponies. Do you think you could venture to let me drive you, and protect your delicate face from the brightness of the day?"

"Why, as far as safety of life and limb are concerned, I certainly think I could," she replied with an enchanting smile. "But—"

"But what?" Alfred asked eagerly. "What else can you fear?"

Again, Miss Thorwold's eyes were fixed upon his. "I'm quite sure you must know what I mean."

She raised the nosegay to her face, concealing every part of it but her eyes.

"Nonsense!" whispered Alfred. He drew a faded leaf from the nosegay.

"Indisputable," said Miss Thorwold, shaking her head.

"And will you be so influenced?"

"Impossible to help it!"

"Damnation!" muttered Alfred. "But you cannot suppose I can endure this?"

"It is not my fault," she smiled. "It is very unfair you should be angry with me."

"I could never be angry with you," Alfred admitted.

Mrs. Dermont spied her son and Miss Thorwold in each other's confidence across the table. There was something endearing in the manner in which her beloved son was engaging himself, but the rest of the party might think it odd if they sat any longer. The courage to interrupt them was found in her knowledge that they might renew their conversation at the drawing room table, or over the pianoforte, or over the knitting which Miss Thorwold might later employ.

She stood up at last. "I hope everyone might enjoy the morning as they like, until we meet again for luncheon. Afterward, the close carriage and park phaeton will come around, in case any of you should like to explore."

The party began to separate. Mrs. Stephens put her arm through Celestina's and invited her into her bedroom. The colonel proposed Mr. Stephens walk around the pastures and see their prodigiously beautiful sheep. Mrs. Dermont told Miss Verepoint that she always gave an hour or two to her knitting in the drawing room, to which Miss Verepoint said she would fetch her knitting and join her.

Miss Thorwold stood and buttoned her lemon colored glove, preparing to follow the other ladies out of the room.

"Can you play billiards?" Alfred asked her.

"Oh no! I do not know the game at all!" she lied. She had, with the most extraordinary perseverance, allowed young men to act as her instructor in any house with a billiard table since the age of seventeen.

"Let me teach you, then," he implored. "I will make you a proficient in under half a dozen lessons!"

She raised a delicate eyebrow and shook her head. "It is impossible, you know, to go to the billiard room with you alone."

Alfred's eyes darted in the direction of Julia, who stood at the window looking out towards the lawn.

"Julia!" he called. "Julia, do make Miss Thorwold go to the billiard room with us! Is it not a particularly pleasant morning room, Julia? Do tell her, will you, what a delightful amusement it is!"

The idea of being the third to their party was certainly not agreeable to poor Julia, but she did want to gain the affection of the beautiful Amelia. "I hope you will not refuse our petition, Miss Thorwold. Do come. I am quite sure it will amuse you."

Miss Thorwold looked to the half-blown beauty of Julia Drummond, who stood before her in a sober-colored silk morning frock. The dress was devoid of any ornament save a neatly stitched cambrie collar and cuffs. Her black hair was smoothly parted and its curling ends were kept in order behind little ears. Not a single ring set off the beauty of her delicate hands, which were covered in nothing more than plain black gloves. Miss Thorwold believed she looked too ridiculously young to be brought into company at all, and so stupidly innocent that it would be impossible to have her as a diverting companion. Still, she could see this creature was in the confidence of Alfred, which might prove useful.

Miss Thorwold accepted the invitation, taking her arm. "You must positively let me make you my friend and companion while I'm here, Miss Drummond."

The billiards went on in the morning, the rides, drives, and walks after midday, and the waltzing every evening. Alfred had no perfectly favorable opportunity to propose the lady of his choice, but Amelia had orchestrated this herself—hoping to postpone the inevitable until her experiment upon the heart of Lord William Hammond had been made.

"I knew what it would come to," she said on her last night of conference with Mrs. Knight. "I know his youthful ardor a great deal too well to trust in his discretion, were he to ask now. You will please remember the terms of our agreement, Mrs. Knight. I am to have one more trial with Lord William. How is that to be managed if Master Dermont is to come to your fete, considering himself as my affianced husband? I will not trust him, I promise you."

"Heaven grant that you will not play your game as you have played it before, Amelia. It is my duty to remind you that it is rather too late for you to run any risk. We leave to return to Crosby tomorrow, and I confess, I have no hope that you will ever encounter such an opportunity again."

"I told you not so long ago, that I do not intend to let this sweet youth come to a formal proposal of marriage until I am satisfied with one more opportunity with Lord William. And now, my dear Mrs. Knight, I tell you again. Be so good as to believe me this time, will you?"

"And what of the young Miss Drummond?" Mrs. Knight inquired. "When we all leave tomorrow, do you trust the fresh faced creature with your young squire? To nurse him through the loneliness of your departure?"

Miss Thorwold laughed. "My dear Mrs. Knight, you should know I would not have left any door open on that account. I have managed to create a wedge between the two confidantes. Just this morning I practically burst into tears, confessing to Alfred that I did not believe Miss Drummond cared for me. He, of course, denied it emphatically—to which I stated I was certain she had looked crossly towards me on more than one occasion. It was all that needed to be done to plant the seed. It will sprout on its own, without my assistance in nurturing it."

After breakfast the next morning, the party bore the breaking up of their extended visit better than might have been expected. All felt strongly about the great advantage of such an intimate, long visit at the Mount, but also felt it was a dreadfully heavy business to live from morning to night under the influence of Mrs. Dermont's incessant civilities. Most were also weary of the colonel's continual pointing out that his house and horses, his grass and sheep, his dogs and guns, and his gardens and stables, were all better than those possessed by any other living gentleman anywhere.

Miss Thorwold knew it her duty to look sweetly sad, which she did effectively. And so, Miss Thorwold and Mrs. Knight departed, leaving Alfred with the delighted hope of soon becoming the happy husband of the best and loveliest woman in the world.

# Chapter 11

The Lords Ripley and William Hammond did not arrive at Crosby on the day of the archery meeting, nor on the day before—but one day earlier still, according to the invitations they had received. Mrs. Knight was well acquainted with Lord Ripley's admirable taste in all things regarding a gala. She naturally thought that the wisest, most prudent course of action would be to take advantage of his talents.

The two gentlemen arrived just in time to dress for dinner. The evening was exceedingly agreeable, for they all appeared in good humor, and perfectly well disposed to be amiable. Lord Ripley, like Mrs. Knight, had long ago given up all hope of Amelia becoming Lady William Hammond. After a quick discussion with Mrs. Knight, he agreed it would be best to enlighten Lord Hammond on the certainty of Amelia's hoped for marriage, in order to prevent his putting himself too conspicuously forward when the young man arrived.

"I say, Hammond, we all know what winning ways you have, and how capable you are of making fair ladies forget there is anybody present but you. This is all vastly well while we are here alone, but I must inform you, that the day after tomorrow you will have the honor of being introduced to a certain Mr. Alfred Dermont. He is a well born youth with a handsome estate, and he aspires to the hand of my fair niece. I am so well pleased by this news, that I fully intend to pinch myself a little, in order to make Amelia a present of a few thousand on the happy occasion. So I give you warning, noble sir, that I shall take it particularly ill if you were to fill the young man's head with jealous fears. I want no risk on this matrimonial prospect. Do you understand?"

"Oh, perfectly, my lord!" Hammond replied.

His tone was as light and airy, but Amelia saw that he changed color. When Lord Ripley returned to his game of chess with Mrs. Knight, she had the unspeakable happiness of receiving a furious glance from his expressive eyes. He got up, and walked out of the room.

Amelia felt certain her experiment had been answered, her delight only tempered by a feeling of reproach for never having tested his attachment before. She looked to Mrs. Knight and Lord Ripley, who were engrossed in their game, and ventured to get up to follow him.

"You drive me to strange manners, my lord, in order to obtain five minutes with you," she said, coming upon him unexpectedly from under the shadow of the portico.

"The driving does not come from me, madam," he replied, with a good deal of solemnity.

"Upon my word, Lord William, it would be quite absurd if on a night as fine as this one, we can only quarrel. Considering the time since I saw you last, you have made great haste to grow disagreeable."

"The time has been long enough, Miss Thorwold, to enable you to do a great deal of business. Permit me to wish you joy."

"It is very strange, Lord William, that the only man with the power to know how far from joy I am, would be the first to utter the mocking word to me."

"Was this why, Miss Thorwold, you invited me to make my appearance here? To have me told what you well knew would stab me in the heart? Was this generous, Amelia?"

"Would it had been more generous, Lord William, to not give you notice of the misery which threatened me until it was too late?" she replied, trembling with anxiety for his answer. "Is that what I ought to have done?"

He took her hand. "No, Amelia, no! The stroke which has stunned me now might have killed me then. But why is it necessary I should hear such tidings at all, if what you have said is true? If you contemplate this hateful marriage with dislike, why have you submitted to such an arrangement? And knowing you had already submitted, how could you ask me to come to witness it?"

"Why have I done this, my lord? Why have I wished to see you once more? Can you really ask me this?"

"But if your feelings, lovely Amelia, are in truth what you might lead me to hope, why have you consented to accept this detestable alliance? Why had you not the courage to refuse him?"

Miss Thorwold had to draw her handkerchief and use it, or seem to use it, before she could give any reason at all. "It is very far from my inclination, Lord William, to say anything to throw blame on my uncle. Unfortunately, it is also impossible to answer your question without it. I was left, as I believe you know, an orphan. I am under his sole care and protection, and he has been, with only one exception, kind and indulgent. That one exception has been the torment of my life. I have had many advantageous proposals of marriage, and have been permitted to refuse them all. But it seems now that Lord Ripley has grown weary of the charge, for on hearing of Mr. Dermont's splendid proposal, he has come down with all his authority. He has made it clear that if I refuse to accept this young man, he shall send me to board with an old spinster cousin of my mother's in North Wales. All I could obtain was permission to postpone giving my final answer until after Mrs. Knight's fete. Can you wonder now, Hammond, why I should wish to see you once more?"

Miss Thorwold wept as she murmured these words, permitting Lord William's arm to steal around her waist. When she did not pull away, he drew her towards him and kissed her on the lips.

"Marry me, Amelia," he whispered. "If you have promised yourself to nobody as of now, promise yourself to me."

"Yes," she cried. "Yes, I will marry you!"

They held each other for a moment, before Amelia insisted they must return to the drawing room.

"You must first promise me, Amelia, not to inform Mrs. Knight what has passed between us," he said urgently. "You must not tell anyone until I have had the opportunity to open my heart to you regarding one or two particular circumstances. Tomorrow after breakfast, we will go for a walk on the grounds. After that, you will be at liberty to report this proposal to both your uncle and Mrs. Knight."

She promised to comply, and for the first time, Lord William Hammond looked at her as his affianced wife. There was a passionately tender triumph in her fine eyes, and a smile of newborn happiness on her lips.

Mrs. Knight was roused to attention by the glowing entrance of Amelia into the drawing room. Although she had a strong suspicion that all her predictions had proved false, she refused to believe it until Amelia herself had told her in her own words. She was dying with impatience, and the tea, wine, and biscuits were all hurried over and dispatched with unusual speed, so that Mrs. Knight and Miss Thorwold found themselves standing at the top of the stairs, each with a bed candle in her hand.

"What have you to tell me, Amelia?" Mrs. Knight asked in an eager whisper. "Shall I come with you into your room, or will you follow me to mine?"

"Neither, my dearest Mrs. Knight," replied Amelia. "I do assure you that I know nothing as yet. In short, there is nothing for me to say to you tonight, except that I am not absolutely without hope. You must engage Lord Ripley tomorrow morning. If you will manage Hammond and I to have a walk in the gardens tomorrow, I may have something to tell you then. I have much to think on, my dear friend, so give me a kiss and wish me goodnight!"

The asked for kiss was given and received in the most affectionate manner.

# Chapter 12

The appointed meeting, which was to afford the affianced lovers their promised talk, was kept. Lord William was the first to arrive at the pretty little grove. There was a root house in the center of it, with a marble headstone erected to the memory of a favorite dog.

"My loveliest Amelia!" he exclaimed, extending his arm and leading her to a sheltered seat. "I must tell you, I must absolutely warn you, my dearest love, that my offering myself in marriage to you is an act utterly devoid of common sense. I hope and trust, my sweet friend, that you already know I am, in the fashionable phrase, an absolute beggar. I do not believe that the son of an English duke would actually be forced, with his wife and family, into a workhouse. Nor do I think it is at all in the ordinary course of things, I fancy, that the niece of a viscount should do so either. It is upon this sort of mysterious dependence, loveliest, that we must rest, for I know of no other."

Amelia dropped her head upon his shoulder. "It does not matter. Such dependence as you speak of, my dear lord, mysterious as you may think it, is a thousand times more dependable than the poor little gentry income of one or two thousand a year, perhaps. All the world might be ready to declare that this sum ought to be enough, but we both know it cannot possibly be enough for people of any real fashion. If you are ready to take the chance of keeping our noble heads above water, I am too."

Lord William took possession of his affianced bride's hand. "Now then, my dear Amelia, we must speak together rather frankly and rationally. We are people who have taken the desperate resolution of setting off together on a perilous expedition. I shall venture to do so with more confidence of being listened to reasonably, because I feel it impossible I should mistake your motive in marrying me. You must love me for myself, because frankly, I have nothing else to offer."

He gently squeezed her fingers before he continued. "I must tell you, sweetest, that our union must at first be secret."

"Secret?" repeated Miss Thorwold. "I presume you actually mean *private*, my dear lord."

"No, my love," he replied. "I mean very literally what I say. If we marry at all, my sweet Amelia, it must be secretly. We will have our banns lawfully published in one of the large suburban parish churches. Here, even the names of William Hammond and Amelia Thorwold will be read over with scores of others, eliciting no dangerous attention at all. This accomplished, we will marry in the same church. This way, I shall have no fear that any word of it will reach our own circle."

"May I ask you, Lord William," Amelia asked gravely, "what are the reasons for this?"

"The reason, Amelia, is that my ducal brother has taken into his head that I may, if I so please, obtain in marriage the magnificently wealthy hand of Miss Upton Savage."

"Marry you to Miss Upton Savage!" Amelia spat. "Is it possible that your brother can have thought up something so horrible? Why, my dearest Lord William, the creature squints and has an enormous quantity of fiery red hair. Marry Miss Upton Savage? You must be jesting."

"The subject has caused me too much vexation to permit me to jest, my love. But I must correct you on thinking my brother unkind. He knows I have debts of some thousands hanging over me. He knows me well enough too, to be perfectly aware that even if I were capable of marrying Miss Upton Savage, I most certainly would not propose to her without acknowledging my debts. She would not decline my proposal, but would certainly faint on the spot of hearing the amount I owe. And so, Watertown has promised to discharge my debts if I make an offer of marriage to her. He knows once married it would be easy enough to pay him back over time. I feel greatly inclined to accept his offer and have the debts paid off, so we might proceed ourselves without them. We will be married, dear Amelia, in the interval—but if this is to be done, you now understand the dire necessity of its being done secretly."

Miss Thorwold did not reply. In truth, she was dreadfully shocked and disappointed. She certainly loved him as much as she was capable of loving anything, but it could not be denied that the idea of envy she would inspire by becoming his wife had some share in her desire. His debts had no effect on her wish for the connection, for she had faith unbounded in his mysterious power of being protected from poverty—but marrying secretly was to put herself beyond the reach of his influence.

"Will you not speak to me, Amelia?" he asked. "If not, I think it would be better for this conversation to end. Nothing but a passionate attachment could make such a proposal endurable to either of us. I have never seen a woman whom I have admired as much as you, and the proposal I have made, however far it was from what you expected, I feel I have given you proof of love that most might think amounted to madness. I put the question before you very plainly, Amelia. The power to decide is in your hands."

She was too highly finished a woman of the *bon ton* to pronounce a decision immediately, unless absolutely driven to it by necessity, and she therefore replied, "If I feel adverse to accepting this proposal, Lord William, you ought to be aware that it is as much for your sake as for my own. Tell me, dearest friend, might our union not take place under circumstances less objectionable, if it were delayed for a month or two?"

Lord William rose from the seat. "Beyond all question, such delay would show our wisdom. I have only to apologize to have hazarded the proposal that has so clearly shocked and offended you."

Amelia felt a degree of terror at the idea that this offer, so long, so anxiously, so despairingly looked for, should now come to nothing. "Stay Hammond! Please stay! How can you leave me to the fate with which I am threatened? I shall be forced into the arms of that detested man if you do not interfere to prevent it!"

"Interfere, Amelia? Cruel girl! What, then, do you call interference? Have I not offered to you my hand, my name, my rank? Have I not offered all that fate and fortune have left me? And how have you received my offer?"

"Forgive me, dearest!" she cried. "Oh Hammond, must I be the wife of another? Must other arms than yours enclose me?"

This touching appeal was answered by Lord William's raising her to his arms and tenderly embracing her. "Let us not torture ourselves further, my lovely girl. There is one way, and one way only to make you my wife. Say that you will submit, for a while, to hide this lovely form from every eye but mine. Say it and I will not waste even an hour in making the arrangements."

"Oh, William!" she replied. "I have no prudence left. Yes, dearest, yes! I am willing to become your wife as secretly as the nature of the act will permit."

"My adoration, sweetest Amelia, shall be proportionate to the blessing you bestow. And now, let us decide what will be necessary to do in order for me to possess my promised treasure as quickly as possible. Do you think that, in the humor your uncle seems to be in, you could extract thirty or forty pounds from him?

You can do it on the pretense of wanting to refresh your wardrobe for the fetes, which are doubtless to be given in the neighborhood. Do you not think that he would be more than usually generous, Amelia?"

"I think he might," she laughed. "It would be so shocking if I were obliged to appear shabbily dressed before the eyes of my future papa and mama in-law."

"Oh, horrible, my love! In short, I shall depend upon you for a little aid in that line. I will work my brother in the same way. Over and above the liquidation of my debts, he really must assist me in my efforts to make a decent appearance myself. I have no doubt, between the two of us, we shall muster a hundred or two. This will be quite enough, my dear love, to make us supremely happy until these debts of mine are paid. We can start afresh by the aid of our noble and rich relatives."

This last phrase sufficed at once to set to rest her anxieties about her own debts. Once the marriage was made public it would be easy enough to keep her own creditors at bay. She should like to see them making an enemy of Lady William Hammond—niece to Lord Ripley—sister to the Duke of Watertown.

"And now, my fairest, let us come to the particulars about how to arrange this scheme. Tell me, have you any trustworthy friend in London? A humble friend will suit our purpose best. Tell me love, do you know anyone?"

"Indeed, I do," replied Amelia. She remembered her favorite dress merchant, Mrs. Stedworth. "I know one of the very best creatures that lived. She is so affectionately attached to me that I believe there is nothing I could ask her to do that she would refuse."

"Do you think, Amelia, that you could rely upon her? Do you think she could be trusted with a secret upon which so much depends?"

"Indeed, I do! She is a person who gains her living by being considered trustworthy. Should she prove false to us, I have influence enough to ruin her already. I am quite sure we may trust her."

"Gains her living by being considered trustworthy?" Lord William repeated. "What species of trust is it, Miss Thorwold, that ladies of fashion place in a person who exists by keeping their secrets?"

Amelia laughed. "Set your mind at rest, my dear, upon the nature of the confidences existing between poor, dear Mrs. Stedworth and her fashionable friends. Like all the men in the world, we ladies indulge in wasteful extravagance in the article of dress. We judge it more dignified and proper to keep the matter a secret, but for many in the fashionable circle, the bold measure of purchasing an expensive new dress would be impossible without first taking measures to meet the demand on our poor, dear little purses by selling an old one. It is true, upon my honor, and this woman is to whom we all apply to on such occasions."

"I have heard something of the kind before," said Lord William, with a playful smile. "I can easily imagine that such a person would be an exceedingly useful acquaintance. But how do you mean to employ her on this occasion, dearest? Has she a sort of dwelling that might serve us as a temporary residence?"

"Exactly that. Her house is extremely respectable looking. I know also that letting a portion of it is occasionally a source of profit to her. I will be able to take refuge with her when I leave Mrs. Knight. Under our present circumstances, it would not do for me to ask for hospitality from any of my fashionable friends."

"If this woman is as you describe, she will be invaluable to us, Amelia. I will arrange everything relative to our marriage. I will take care to sleep the necessary number of nights in the parish where the banns will be published. Published, dearest, to a parish who shall hear our names and not know who they are. But it is you, my love, who must arrange the mode by which we will elude all eyes and ears for a month or two. I should think the safest thing would be for you to go abroad—for both of us to go abroad, I mean—as soon as we are married. That is, provided you know anyone whom you can mention to your uncle and Mrs. Knight as having invited you."

"It certainly would be best, but I have one objection to it. The truth is, I cannot tell them that I have decided to refuse Mr. Dermont unless I tell them I am to be married to you. I am positive I would never get another sixpence from my uncle otherwise. If I can take them into our confidence, all would be easy enough."

"Impossible," said Lord William flatly. "If you persist in recommending this we must end the whole scheme. I have told you already what ruin will fall upon me if my brother even suspected that I thought of marrying any other but Miss Upton Savage. I cannot, I will not risk this. Swear to me that you will have no other confidant than Mrs. Stedworth, or give me one last kiss and let me leave you forever."

"No, Lord William, no! You shall not leave me. I will promise everything, risk everything, rather than lose you! I swear to you it shall be done."

Lord William took her face in his hands. "I am horribly hard up, my sweet, and you must therefore get what you can from Lord Ripley. I will arrange for a letter to come by post today, obliging me to set off by the mail coach tonight, with an earnest summons from my sick mother. I shall arrive early tomorrow morning in London, where his grace of Watertown still lingers. You get what you can from Lord Ripley, and I will notify you of how we proceed from there."

# Chapter 13

Mrs. Knight's party was like most other parties: delightful to some, displeasing to others, and fatiguing to all. Amelia, however, had an important game to play, and was too happy, too triumphant to feel fatigue.

To Alfred, her conduct was equally safe and prudent. She received him with an air of flattering distinction, and was even politely civil to Julia. The colonel has insisted upon bringing her, despite Julia's earnest assurances that she would rather be at home.

When the enamored young man requested a few minutes private conversation, Amelia begged him to spare her when so many eyes were upon them. "I will not affect to misunderstand you, and I should be sorry to believe that you could misunderstand me—but this is no time to explain ourselves further. I believe we understand each other perfectly, and are in perfect agreement."

To her uncle she had addressed herself with equal skill and success. A draft for fifty pounds was the reward for her assuring him she would marry. The fact that he assumed she meant Mr. Alfred Dermont was not a misunderstanding she felt compelled to correct.

To Mrs. Knight, who had been eager to question her at Lord William's sudden departure, she said, "All doubts about my final destination are at an end now, my dearest. You shall know every particular of my conversation with Lord William, but it must not be now. Were I to go over it with you at this moment, I am quite certain I would be in no state to appear at your fete. Let me assure you, without further discussion of the subject, I have made up my mind to marry with as little loss of time as possible. You may depend upon it, my good friend, that the time will come when I will be delighted to talk over everything in detail. For the present, I shall try to enjoy myself as much as I can."

Mrs. Knight had taken this to mean her friend would become the wife of Mr. Alfred Dermont, as that was vastly more important than any discussion about conversations between Miss Thorwold and Lord William.

The much more difficult business for Miss Thorwold was in announcing and arranging her departure. Lord Ripley had declared his intention of leaving Crosby on the morning after the fete. He, of course, was determined upon his niece remaining there after his departure. The interval was not lost, as the time permitted her to write to Mrs. Stedworth, and to receive her answer, which was in every way what she had wished.

The post which arrived a few hours after her uncle's departure brought not only Mrs. Stedworth's letter, but another which Amelia made sure to open in the presence of Mrs. Knight.

"What have you got there, Amelia?" Mrs. Knight asked.

"I have received quite unpleasant news," Miss Thorwold replied. "My poor friend, Caroline Marchmont, is in a dangerous state. Her lungs are thought to be affected and I believe they are going to take her abroad. Poor, dear girl! I cannot help but feel this to be a heavy misfortune at such a moment. She is the only person of my age that I have ever formed any real intimacy with. I am quite determined to go with her for a little while, my marriage finally settled. It is a great disappointment to me."

Mrs. Knight very nearly laughed, and Miss Thorwold looked at her with indignation. "I have always thought," she said bitterly, "that a girl so young and lovely as Caroline was unlikely to be a favorite with you, Mrs. Knight. I know that female youth and beauty are not likely what you would pet most, but I must confess, I did not quite expect so very unfeeling a mark of your apathy as you have now given. I shall be much obliged to walk on the grounds or remain alone in my own room for the rest of the evening."

"Upon my word, Amelia, you are being ridiculous," returned Mrs. Knight. "I have heard you abuse Carolyn Marchmont a hundred times. But pray do not let us quarrel. Please do take your walk or a rest in your room if you prefer it right now to my poor drawing room."

Miss Thorwold rose without a reply and walked out of the room.

It was rather later than usual on the following morning when Mrs. Knight entered the breakfast parlor.

"Let Miss Thorwold know that breakfast is ready," she said.

The man who received this command returned to the breakfast room with a look of astonishment. He handed a salver to his mistress with a letter upon it. "Miss Thorwold is not to be found, ma'am. This note, ma'am, was on her dressing table."

"That horrid girl was born to be my torment!" she cried, unfolding the note.

*I can scarcely imagine anything, Mrs. Knight, that could induce me to risk that most vulgar of all adventures—a quarrel. I am afraid no extent of ladylike philosophy can soothe our tempers and prevent us to meet when we are rude or unfeeling. To avoid a repetition of this, I have determined to leave your house to protect against suffering in the same way in future. I have no intention of sacrificing your pleasant company forever, so please do not for an instant think this is the case. I will visit the friend whose illness caused your mirth, and shall likely accompany her abroad for a few weeks. The matrimonial prospects opening before me will, of course, account for the tone of independence as to my movements. Please explain properly to the family at the Mount the cause of my*

*sudden departure. I sincerely hope we may meet again under*
*circumstances that will enable us both to forget the disagreeable*
*scene which caused our separation.*

> *Yours, with unfailing consideration,*
> *Amelia Thorwold*

After a few inquiries, it was easily determined that Miss Thorwold had left the house—her trunks already sent for—and taken the omnibus to the London railroad. Mrs. Knight had sent and received a rushed correspondence of her own, which was met with confirmation of Miss Marchmont's illness. Still, Mrs. Knight was in a state of tormenting uncertainty regarding Miss Thorwold's real motives. She would not accept that Miss Thorwold had been so deeply concerned for Miss Caroline Marchmont, and that such offense would be taken when the display of concern was met with a laugh.

Mrs. Knight could only believe that Amelia, having made up her mind to marry Mr. Alfred Dermont, was simply taking advantage of last night's disagreement to release herself for a week or two of freedom. She felt it was not unlikely that Miss Thorwold might think a week or two passed on the continent would be better than anymore long visitations to the Mount. On this point, Mrs. Knight was well disposed to agree with her. It was fair to let her indulge on this last little time to herself with impunity.

She ordered her carriage and made her way to the Mount. As she approached the house, she saw young Alfred Dermont beneath the trees not far from the road. Aware she would have a much better chance of learning how matters really stood from the young man than from his mother, she immediately stopped the carriage and joined him.

"You come alone?" he asked.

"Yes, I am alone, my dear Alfred," she said with an affectionate familiarity. "There is nothing to cause uneasiness about my dear Amelia's absence."

She put her arm under his in a show of sisterly intimacy. "You must forgive me if I have taken too much for granted, dear Alfred, what I so ardently desire to be true. Tell me, am I right in believing that you love my darling Amelia?"

"Love her, Mrs. Knight?" he asked. "Do I love her? Oh, yes. Yes, I most certainly do love her. I adore her! But why are you alone? The last words Amelia said to me at Crosby were consenting to listen to me favorably. It was my hope, this very day, to throw myself at her feet and tell her what she knows already."

"And your parents, dear? Do they unite their wishes with yours?"

"My dearest Mrs. Knight, I have no secrets hidden from them and they share my hopes. But why are you alone?" he pressed anxiously.

Mrs. Knight explained with touching description the strong affection Amelia had for her poor, failing friend. "She was forced by her love of Miss Marchmont, dear Alfred, to tear herself away from you at a time when a happy life of mutual affection was opening before her. To tear herself away at such a moment is what few creatures would have the courage to do. But our Amelia Thorwold is a noble being!"

Alfred and Mrs. Knight indulged themselves for a few minutes longer on their mutual admiration and affection for the divine Amelia. They entered the house together, arm in arm, with an air of confidential, good understanding.

"I have just a few words I'd like to say to the colonel and Mrs. Dermont, by themselves," she said.

Colonel Dermont led the way to his library, and the trio remained shut up in there until Mrs. Knight had managed to learn the exact amount of Colonel Dermont's income. He also disclosed the noble allowance of half the annual income he meant to settle immediately upon his son: a generous five hundred a year pin money, and fifteen hundred per year jointure. Having heard all of this, it was impossible Mrs. Knight could ever be more assured, save the performance of the marriage ceremony itself, that the match between Alfred Dermont and Miss Thorwold was completely settled and arranged. She took her leave confident that her letter to Lord Ripley detailing these facts, even with news of Amelia's departure, would be well received.

Julia and Alfred had been in the drawing room, Julia making a move to leave as soon as she saw Mrs. Knight pass through the hall.

"Oh Julia, do not go," he said. "I know I have been angry with you, for you were harsh to my Amelia, but in this happy moment I can no longer bear my dear, adopted sister should look upon me so coldly. Forgive me, dearest Julia! Forgive us both if we have misconstrued your manner. My sweet Amelia was wounded because she wished you to love her, and she felt you did not. Look at me as you used to, Julia, or I shall scarcely be able to feel quite happy. And I am happy, Julia! I have just been told on excellent authority that Amelia loves me!"

Julia closed her eyes and felt in her heart a wish, a wish that she might never open them again. Something in the words and manner of Alfred were so different from anything she had seen before. The heedless, reckless tone of the spoiled boy was completely gone. Instead, there was a softness so new, so touching, and so terrible, that to bear it all with proper composure seemed totally beyond her power.

She opened her eyes to see Alfred staring at her. She saw the unspeakable comfort of his features showing no trace of him guessing what was passing in her heart.

"My dearest Alfred, I suffer from nothing more than a painful toothache," she lied. "If you fancy that I have either looked or spoken to Miss Thorwold as if I were cross, you must forgive me. I do wish you every happiness, my dearest Alfred, but if you knew how dreadfully painful it is for me to speak at all, I am quite sure you would not wish me to talk about it now."

Julia said all this with such persuasion, that Alfred had not the least doubt that she was, and had been, suffering dreadfully from a toothache.

# Chapter 14

Considering Miss Thorwold had never traveled before without an attendant, she suffered little inconvenience in transferring herself from Crosby to Mrs. Stedworth's house on Half Moon Street, Piccadilly. Miss Thorwold had, for many years, been an excellent customer to Mrs. Stedworth. She had also been an amiable young lady, one whom Mrs. Stedworth confided in, and one who valued her without allowing her buying and selling position in society to interfere with their friendship.

Mrs. Stedworth was reliable and had the peculiar gift of *tact*. It was by means of this that she had been able to bring some of her proudest customers to treat her as a favored friend and counselor, and not just as a dealer in second hand finery. This nicety of tact, amassed over years by Mrs. Stedworth, assisted in displaying the profound courtesy with which Miss Thorwold was received at the bottom of the stairs. She composed herself with the appearance of having stood awaiting the honor of Miss Thorwold's presence for hours, and received the young lady's extended hand with extreme modesty. This suggested to Amelia that Mrs. Stedworth was so occupied with thinking of her as the future Lady William Hammond, that she had quite forgotten the easy terms they used to be upon.

Mrs. Stedworth was kindly determined to put Miss Thorwold at ease. There was too much to be done to afford wasting time on ceremony. Mrs. Stedworth had sufficient good sense to agree that the rank of Lord William more than compensated for the loss of the young squire, and the seeming imprudence of Miss Thorwold's present enterprise. Amelia felt the greatest confidence in Mrs. Stedworth and determined to avail herself to her advice and assistance throughout the whole affair.

Lord William made his appearance at Half Moon Street just at the moment that his lovely Amelia was ready to receive him. She looked so magnificently beautiful that he declared, "Not even at the famous ball at Almack's where I first beheld you, did you look so divinely lovely as you do at this moment."

Miss Thorwold took this compliment with a heavy dose of relief. She was by no means ignorant to the instability of love affairs with men of high fashion. The prompt arrival of Lord William gave comfort that his love had evidently increased, rather than diminished, by the near prospect of calling her his wife.

Mrs. Stedworth had perceived when the young lady first arrived, that she was not without some lingering doubts about her noble lover's faith. She saw these doubts quickly wear away. With each day, she spoke with greater confidence of the happy and brilliant future opening before her as the wife of one of the most admired noblemen in England.

Mrs. Stedworth was exceedingly pleased that it should be so, and was not without personal hopes of her own. She knew the Watertown family sufficiently well by reputation to think it possible, with a good introduction, that she might hope for some profitable dealings as a result of it.

A fortnight later at the vastly inelegant suburban church, Mrs. Stedworth stood faithfully beside Miss Thorwold while a gentleman clothed in a dirty surplice performed the marriage ceremony. A person brought to the church by Lord William had the honor of giving the bride away. He was unknown to Amelia, and when she asked her noble bridegroom the name of his shy friend, he only replied, "You don't know him, my love. He is an excellent fellow and greatly attached to me. His name is Morrison."

The happy pair took their bridal tour to a romantic and retired village in Gloucestershire. The widowed mistress of the pretty rustic in where they lodged was also called Morrison. Though neither elegant nor costly, the inn was scrupulously neat and comfortable. There was little to distinguish their honeymoon from that of any others, save that it lasted only a fortnight. Lady William had the satisfaction of knowing that the curtailment of their honeymoon was not a matter of choice, but of necessity.

"My angel!" Lord William exclaimed, as they sat together for their twelfth breakfast.

"My angel!" he exclaimed again, presenting her with a twelfth nosegay of moss rosebuds gathered from the garden. "How utterly impossible it will be for me to believe that any other man could be as supremely blessed as I have been. But alas, my love, how swift do such moments vanish! Can you believe, my Amelia, that we have already been married a fortnight?"

"The time has flown swiftly, my dear lord," replied her ladyship. "The hours have been too precious for me not to count. I know quite well, Lord William, that we have been married a whole fortnight."

"I am sadly obliged to remember, and you must remember too, my love, that it is absolutely necessary we should return immediately to town. I must find out whether Watertown has redeemed his promise by paying my alarming debts, for until I have this assurance, I can only creep about like an escaped felon by owl's light."

A slight shade of anxiety swept across Lady William Hammond's face. "You have no doubt, my love, about his having kept his promise, have you?"

His lordship replied gaily, "It is a sin, dearest, to doubt the pledged word of a noble duke. Nevertheless, it behooves me as a man of business to confirm this fact without delay. It would be rather awkward, most beautiful Amelia, were there to be any mistake about it."

"Will his grace of Watertown be a good deal disappointed when he discovers that he has paid the money for nothing? That is to say, without having obtained the wealthy sister he so coveted?"

"Upon my word, dear love, I have not taken the trouble to consider it. All I have considered is that I am as much the lawful son of the late duke as he. If he suffers me to be marched to jail, he will be disgraced for life. This is the only rational light in which to view the transaction between us. As for him daring to resent my choice of a wife, I will not suppose it possible."

The breakfast was finished as all their former breakfasts had been, with a walk through the hay fields by the side of the river. The sun had not set when they left the white washed inn of Mrs. Morrison far behind them, taken away at great pace upon the railroad that brought them into London early the following morning.

# Chapter 15

From the perfect reconciliation which had taken place between herself and Alfred, Julia was enjoying as much happiness as seemed likely to fall to her lot. She was as equally relieved by the absence of Amelia as Alfred was in his suffering from it. Julia listened for long hours to the rhapsodies of Alfred's love for another. She did this with such gentle martyr-like endurance, there were almost moments in which she forgave herself for the sin of having loved too well—from an honest consciousness that the penance she endured was sufficient to atone for it.

In this manner, days and weeks passed on to the annoyance of the enamored young man. There was nothing to suggest to either his parents or himself any shadow of a doubt concerning the ultimate success of his passion.

Lord Ripley owed a considerable debt of gratitude to the friendly exertions of Mrs. Knight, who continued to make the prolonged absence of Amelia appear to the Dermont family as no more than an additional reason to love her. Her exemplary kindness in attending the sickbed of her young friend was, again and again, applauded.

Mrs. Knight found nothing surprising in Amelia's silence towards her. They had quarreled and she didn't expect to hear from her again until such a time as she should be ready to return to her accustomed apartment at Crosby.

There had also been a military movement in Overby. The old encampment of Major Sommerton had been ordered off, and a new regiment installed. This change was the most important public event to befall Overby and its neighborhood in the six weeks since the departure of Miss Thorwold from Crosby. Although it arrived among gloom and sadness at the loss of Captain Waters, Ensign Wheeler, and a host of other favorites, a considerable degree of unexpected brilliance was the consequence. The principle cause was that the regiment of which this new detachment made a part was favored with the aristocracy of England. No less than three noble scions of right noble houses were among the officers now sent to keep the working men of the district in order.

A series of dinner parties immediately began, which soon led to a better acquaintance between the three honorables and the gentlefolk of the county families. Mrs. Knight declared that it did her quite good to speak to somebody who knew something about the rest of the world. Mrs. Verepoint had the gratification of discovering one of these honorable men was the son of an intimate friend. Colonel Dermont was startled at being informed, within two months of their arrival, that the Honorable Mr. Borrowdale had no wish so near to his heart as to lay it at the feet of his little ward, Julia.

This was a proposal so every way advantageous that the colonel could not be anything but extremely pleased by it. Nevertheless, his first and foremost powerful sensation on receiving Mr. Borrowdale's letter was surprise. Up until that moment, Julia had been considered so completely a child by all of them, that the notion of her being married was almost laughable. Of course, he knew better than to treat such a proposal lightly. He communicated the matter to his wife with a great deal of dignity.

"What can you mean by talking such nonsense, colonel?" Mrs. Dermont cried. "What joke have you in your head now?"

Julia had grown rapidly during the last half year. This additional height had increased both her beauty and her air of womanhood. At seventeen minus a month or two, the heart-struck Mr. Borrowdale found her to be exceptionally lovely. Alfred was scarcely more aware that she was beautiful than his parents. On hearing of Mr. Borrowdale's proposal, his surprise was fully as great as theirs.

"Alfred, don't you agree this is a capital good match for her?" the colonel asked.

"Upon my word, sir, I know nothing at all about it," he replied. "The young man is so completely a stranger to us all, that it seems quite impossible we should be capable of forming an opinion of him. And Julia herself, who of course it most dearly concerns, is still so completely a child as to render the asking her to form any serious judgment on the subject an absolute farce."

"Why, to be sure, Julia is rather young, Alfred. But it is a capital good connection, and I don't feel as if I should be doing right to refuse it just because Julia happens to be a child in our hearts. There are many girls who marry at seventeen, and I won't allow her to marry until after her seventeenth birthday, when she comes of age. That will make all the settlement work so much more straightforward and simple. I don't think the dear child will be in any such hurry herself, as to make her wish to marry him before then."

"Then Julia has accepted him, sir?" Alfred asked.

"I look at it as a matter of course that she will accept him," the colonel replied. "Borrowdale is by far the handsomest young man she has seen, except yourself—and you count for nothing, Alfred. Even if she were years older the poor child could never have looked on you in any other light than a brother. I can't say there is much danger in her refusing him. However, I haven't had the opportunity of asking her yet, for she was out walking when the note came. She has not been in since."

"I would like to be present when you tell her of it," said Alfred.

"Then I will do it at once, for here she comes."

The colonel opened the parlor door and placed himself on the steps of the hall.

"Come with me, my dear, will you?" he asked, holding out his hand to her. "I have something to say to you."

Julia's face colored at the summons, certain she was to be told of Miss Thorwold's return and the blessed nuptial to take place.

"Julia, I have some news for you," said the colonel. "I think it will surprise you a little, but I hope it will please you more. I am quite sure it will, if you are the sensible young lady I take you for."

"Well, sir, what is it?" she asked quietly.

The colonel looked at her affectionately. "My dear child, I have to inform you that the Honorable Mr. Borrowdale aspires to the happiness of possessing your fair hand in marriage. He proposes settlements which might satisfy even the most covetous guardian in the world. It is proper I should also tell you, as a matter of delicacy, Mr. Borrowdale's elder brother had a dreadful fall from his horse a year or two ago and is not expected to live. He has been in a miserable state since the accident, and is said to have fallen into a rapid decline. So you may perceive the wife of Mr. Borrowdale is certain of becoming Lady Middlehurst."

"The gentleman's declining state, sir, will not make a difference to me. I do assure you, I certainly shall never marry Mr. Borrowdale," Julia replied.

"And pray, why so, Miss Drummond?" demanded the colonel.

"Because I would rather not, sir," said Julia. "Let us not talk anymore of Mr. Borrowdale, my dear sir. It can be of no use, as I do not want to be married to anybody. I like living at the Mount better than anywhere a thousand times over, and if you and dear Mrs. Dermont will allow me, I shall wish never to go away. I know you will be so kind as to write exactly such in a letter to Mr. Borrowdale. Will you, sir?"

Her coaxing did nothing to restore the colonel's good humor. "The only sort of letter which ought to be written to Mr. Borrowdale is one in which I inform him that his flattering proposal is accepted. We all know it is perfectly impossible so very young a lady as you are, Miss Julia, can have fallen in love with anyone else. It is my duty as your guardian to tell you that so excellent an offer must not be rejected until you have given yourself time to consider it. If I were to sit down at this very moment and write the answer you have told me to do, I have little doubt that you would reproach me for it before this time tomorrow. Do you not think so, Alfred?"

Alfred replied eagerly, "No, indeed sir, I do not. I must say I shall think you very wrong if you refuse to write in the manner Miss Drummond desires. If she is old enough to accept an offer of marriage, she must also be old enough to refuse one. I really cannot conceive that you can, in any way, be justified in refusing, or even delaying, to forward Julia's answer to Mr. Borrowdale."

Tears, which Alfred felt sure were of gratitude, started to pour from Julia's eyes on hearing him take her part. She gave him a look of thankfulness as she passed into the hall and made her escape.

"If that is really your opinion, Alfred," said the colonel, "I certainly shall give up my own. It does seem a pity to refuse such an excellent offer. You certainly cannot expect she will ever receive better. With all my care, I am sure, her fortune will be but a trifle beyond ten thousand pounds. Even in these poor days, that will not suffice to purchase a coronet. Neither must we reckon too much on her beauty. I don't think anybody ever did think her pretty before. I can't say I think her plain myself, rather the contrary, especially of late. But that is no rule for others and I never did hear anyone call her handsome. All this ought to be taken into consideration, you know, or I shall not be doing my duty as a guardian."

"I do not think, sir," returned Alfred, rather thoughtfully, "that Julia is ugly enough to be urged, on that account, to marry anybody she does not like."

"I do not mean to say she is ugly," said the colonel. "You know well enough, Alfred, that I never do refuse to listen to your opinion. Still, I do think it a great pity."

The refusal was written, and there was an end to the affair. The young honorable obtained a leave of absence for a few months, with the well formed hope that the detachment would be changed before he was due to return.

Julia was grateful to Alfred for his timely interference, as it certainly saved her from a good deal of trouble. Had Mrs. Dermont been consulted before the answer was dispatched, she would not have been let off so easily. Alfred was rewarded speedily for his good deed, for the next day he received news of his beautiful Amelia—and it reached him in what most felt to be the most flattering manner in the world.

# Chapter 16

By the end of her second week spent on Half Moon Street, Lord William had not yet given Amelia any hope to believe she might be approaching the end of the hateful incognito under which she was living. On the thirty-second day after he had saluted her beautiful lips as his bride, Lord William returned to their private lodgings at Mrs. Stedworth's for dinner.

Amelia had decided she would neglect her appearance, on purpose, to show him he was not to go on forever expecting that she should please him. She would let him see what the effects of his inattention and her hiding had in the most visible way possible. Amelia's hair, to which she usually paid the very greatest attention, had been completely ignored. As it was not her custom to wear it in the convenient fashion of bands, but in long ringlets, the absence of care produced the deplorable effect of limp, lifeless strands blanketing her face. The daring neglect of her rouge was more fatal still, for all luster seemed to have faded from her eyes, and a heavy look of sullen discontent took its place.

The first words uttered by his lordship upon entering the drawing room and seeing his greatly altered lady were, "The Devil!"

There was so much genuine astonishment in his look and manner, Amelia determined she would take advantage of it. "Your coming here to swear at me, my lord, will not go far towards persuading me that I am doing my duty towards myself and my noble relatives by remaining here. Believe me at once when I tell you that I have had enough of it. Has you brother paid your debts, my lord? You gave me to understand that was in your power to make happen as soon as we returned to town. If this will be done, I am willing to go abroad with you, but it must be as your wife, sir, and not as your mistress. Nor do I doubt my uncle will assist us in living decently abroad until you gain possession of your mother's fortune. Are your debts paid, Lord William?"

Lord William never took his eyes off her while she was speaking. Coolly, he replied, "What on earth have you been doing to yourself, Amelia? You look grotesque and forty years old, at the very least. What does it all mean? Are you getting up a comedy for my amusement?"

"Far from it, my lord," she replied. "We certainly have been amusing ourselves with comedy, but it is over. You must be aware that for a woman of fashion I have had enough of it. Has your brother paid your debts, my lord?"

"No, my lady, he has not."

"Is he about to do it?" she pressed.

Lord William continued to stare at her, expressionless.

"Is he about to do it?' she repeated. "Speak sir. I shall endure this child's play no longer."

"Do you think the dinner is nearly ready?" he asked, his voice as void of expression as his features.

In that moment, Mrs. Stedworth's maid entered with their dinner. She had the honor of filling the joint post of butler and footman, preventing the conversation from continuing. Her ladyship, however, was not silent. She found fault in everything, in a manner she never had before, with the dishes, the plates, the knives, the forks, the spoons, the glasses, the tablecloth, and the napkins.

The silence of his lordship only fueled her frustration, and Amelia's tirade continued.

When they were again alone, Amelia immediately took advantage of the circumstance, expressing her extreme weariness of the life she was leading. She pointed out her determination to put an end to it directly, by either writing to, or seeing, the Duke of Watertown. She would inform him, as well as all her friends and other acquaintance, of her marriage.

Lord William had his eyes fixed on her the whole time, but rather as a man critically examining a painting, than one listening to the complaints of his wife.

"Upon my honor, my lord, I think you would show infinitely more common sense if you would converse with me, instead of staring at my pale face and undressed hair. Have no fears, my lord, that the wife you chose will disgrace you in the circles we are both accustomed to moving in. Nature has done a good deal for me, and I have no scruples in promising to manage the rest, as I always have, when I find myself in a situation where it is worth my while. Tell me, Lord William, when is it your intention to take me from this detestable lodging, and to a place either in this country or any other, in a position more befitting your wife? Answer me this question, my lord, and I shall then know what it is my duty to do."

There was a solitary bottle of claret wine on the table. Lord William took it up, and asked with a gentlemanly air, "May I offer you some wine, Amelia?"

She did not refuse it. On the contrary, she advanced her glass towards him. He filled it, then his own.

"To your health," he said. He swallowed the wine, quietly rose from his chair, turned to look back at her for half an instant, and left the room.

"Wretch!" she shouted, making her way to the door. She paused as she stepped to the passage, realizing she was in no state to meet the eyes of anyone—even her trusted landlady. The house door shut with a thud that made itself heard over the greater part of the house. Amelia retreated back into her room. As the hours wore away, she took coffee, and then tea, and then a novel, and then her bed. Her spirits recovered their usual calmness, and she went quietly to sleep.

When she woke the next morning, the fair Amelia rose and dressed herself. She told the maid servant who brought in her breakfast to inform her mistress that she desired to speak with her. The message was promptly delivered and as promptly obeyed, and Amelia, once more, found herself seated with her confidante, Mrs. Stedworth.

# Chapter 17

Mrs. Stedworth took a seat in a chair Amelia waved her towards to occupy, fixing her eyes on her ladyship with the air of a person intent on listening to all that was going to be said.

"Now then, let me tell you how I am situated," said Amelia. "The secrecy, which, as you know—"

Before she could finish, she was interrupted by the entrance of the servant of the house, who stepped rapidly towards her. She put a letter into Amelia's hand. The address was in the handwriting of her husband, and it occurred to her that he had probably left it himself.

"How did this come?" she asked the maid.

While waiting for the girl's answer she broke the seal. Though occupied by her own affairs, she was struck by the girl's countenance. Her whole aspect, which was usually gentle and pleasing, had now something uncomfortable in it that she could not understand.

"Do you not hear me? Where did you get this letter?" she asked again.

"I got it from the gentleman that is just gone out," replied the girl. Her face flushed red.

"What gentleman?" demanded Amelia.

"The gentleman that has been lodging here," returned the maid.

"The gentleman that has been lodging here?" repeated Amelia. "Just gone out? You mean just come in, I suppose?"

"No, I don't," the girl said back. She looked to the ground, shifting from one foot to the other.

"You are extremely impertinent to speak and behave in the way you do, you saucy minx," shot Mrs. Stedworth. "Go out of the room this moment."

"Yes I will. And out of this house too," the maid added. "It don't suit me."

Mrs. Stedworth rose and pushed the girl towards the door.

"Away with you then!" she cried. "You got your wages yesterday, so no more need be said. You are a right bad one. Be off! And I will be off to watch you, lest I find myself a few silver spoons poorer!"

The girl burst into tears and Mrs. Stedworth pushed her further into the hall, shutting the door upon Amelia and her letter.

*My dear Miss Thorwold,*

*You are still too lovely a woman for me to ever regret, for your sake, as well as my own, the soft cloud which enveloped us so delightfully. But as it is your will to tear it off, I must submit. Were it not for the wifely tone you took in our last conversation, my beautiful Amelia, I certainly should not think it possible that with your excellent good sense, and knowledge of the world, you could believe the ceremony which passed between us was anything but a farce. That you, my dear creature, could for a moment believe that I, in the sadly embarrassed state of my finances, should run my free neck into the noose of matrimony, with a lady whom I have every reason to believe is as unlike Miss Upton Savage in her purse, as in her features; that you, my lovely Miss Thorwold, should believe this? I freely confess, it does appear to me possible.*

*It would, however, be extremely wrong for me to doubt your word on this subject, and therefore I am bound to believe that you really fancy yourself my wife. If this be so, I must not shrink from the disagreeable task of undeceiving you. You are not my wife, my beautiful Amelia, but you have been to me infinitely dearer than any wife is ever likely to be. It is now evident that the only course left for me is to marry according to my brother's disagreeable wishes. I need say no more, Amelia, on this hateful subject. I am quite sure you will pity me. As to you, my sweet girl, though your conduct and manner last night certainly vexed me a great deal, I do, and ever shall, feel a degree of tender interest for you which must always make your happiness a subject of deep anxiety to me.*

*At this painful moment of parting, it is a great satisfaction to me to remember that you are not committed in the eyes of your friends. A blessing, my dear Miss Thorwold, which is rarely* enjoyed by a single lady in your rank of life, after yielding herself with a little too much facility to the affections of the heart.

Everything, my sweet friend, seems to have favored you. I saw in the papers yesterday that your friend, Caroline Marchmont, has died in Nice. Nothing could be easier for you to take advantage of this most happy coincidence.

I recommend your immediate return to Crosby. I know you have formerly been at Nice, and will therefore be in no danger of being thrown out for not knowing the localities. Return to Mrs. Knight, in mourning, and a good deal out of spirits at the loss of your friend. Then will follow, of course, a full explanation to Colonel Dermont and his family, and the fulfillment of your engagement to the young man. A lover of twenty-one, or rather less, I believe, is easily urged to speed. There are a thousand reasons, my sweet friend, which will make your immediate marriage a most pleasing event to me. I am sorry for the little roughness which took place between us last night. Let it be forgotten, my dear Miss Thorwold, and nothing remembered but the happiness we have enjoyed in each other's company.

And now, I must say adieu! But I see no reason why it should be a lasting one. I have no doubt that your influence over your husband will be omnipotent. If so, you will of course make him bring you to London. Then, Amelia, we may meet again, if you will promise while you are the right side of forty, to never let me see you looking again as you did last night. On my side, I will venture to promise you that nothing could give me greater

*pleasure than being permitted to repeat the assurance of the*
*affectionate esteem with which I now subscribe myself,*

> *Yours, faithfully,*
> *William Hammond*

She rose and rang the bell violently. It was answered by Mrs. Stedworth.

"Nothing the matter ma'am, is there?" she asked.

Amelia handed her the letter. "Read this, Mrs. Stedworth."

Mrs. Stedworth took the letter and went to the window. She read it from beginning to end, a proper proportion of horror and astonishment crossing her face.

"Oh! My dear lady! What can I say to you?" she asked. "Is it possible this terrible letter can be true?"

"Is it possible that you can ask me that question?" Amelia replied. "Are you not able to swear upon your knowledge that it is false? Were you not yourself a witness to the ceremony? Did you not yourself see it performed in a church, and by a clergyman?"

"To be sure I did, my dear young lady! To be sure I did! How could I be such a fool to put faith in such a contemptible falsehood? I am sorry to my heart, my dear lady, that my lord is not a better man. Such as he is, he is your husband, sure enough."

"And that man, Morrison, my dear Mrs. Stedworth? Do you happen to know where he lives or anything about him? My worthless lord gave me to understand that he was an intimate friend of his.—Why do you bite you lip that way? Why do you turn away from me?"

"Never mind me, my dear precious lady!" replied Mrs. Stedworth in agitation. "It is all nonsense, I am quite sure and certain, and you must not mind me. I will set my own mind to rest about it before I lay down to sleep."

"You will drive me mad, Mrs. Stedworth!" cried Amelia. "Do not go on uttering dark hints! Pray do not pretend to fancy that it is a way to spare my feelings. I would rather ten thousand times that you would tell me at once if you think I am not married at all."

"God forbid, my dearest Miss Thorwold—my dearest Lady William, I would say—God forbid I should utter such cruel words! I won't deny, Miss Thor—my lady, I mean—I won't attempt to deny I was struck by the odd look of the clergyman. And now that you speak of that man, Morrison, when I first looked at him I did say to myself, of all the gentlemen I ever saw, he had the least look of one. And as to the dark clerk, he might have been first cousin to the parson as far as his looks went."

"By all which, Mrs. Stedworth, I must presume you mean to express doubts of the reality of my marriage. Speak plainly. Is it not so?"

"I will tell you at once, painful as it is, that the more I think about his lordship's letter, the more afraid I feel it might be true. I will make inquiries, Miss Thorwo—my lady—and I won't rest this night without getting at the truth, whatever it may be."

"You are perfectly right, my dear Mrs. Stedworth. Nothing else can be of use to me. While you have been thinking over the looks of the parson and the clerk, I have been thinking on the real value of Lord William in the capacity of a husband. Truly, these thoughts have not ended in my wishing to keep a fast hold of him. He is a villain of the very blackest dye, but this signifies little. My interest in the matter is how to make this horrible business end with the least injury to me. If we prove the marriage to be a true one, I am Lady William Hammond, that is quite certain. And it is quite certain that being Lady William Hammond is the very thing upon which I had set my heart. I fear the sort of way I might make my appearance as a bride if this wretch chooses to press his story. Its being false will make little difference in the only set I care about. Everybody knows he is a libertine, but I also know there are dozens of women, maids, wives, and widows who would suppose they believe him, whether they did or not. The doubtful Lady William is, therefore, a very doubtful blessing. As to any comfort to be derived from wealth, I happen to know perfectly well that he is not only penniless, but desperately deep in debt."

Amelia fanned herself vehemently. "For all these excellent reasons," she continued, "I do positively declare to you, that I would rather believe the ceremony which united us to be fictitious than real."

"Thank heaven that I hear you say that, dear lady!" replied Mrs. Stedworth. "I shall now set about the work of inquiry with courage. Let it end as it will, but no doubt must be left on the subject."

"A great deal depends upon your being able to prove to me that I am just Amelia Thorwold still. I mean to say that, if I must, I can manage to make all that has happened pass away as if a dream.

My abominable Don Juan will take care to keep silent for his own sake, and you, dear Stedworth, will keep silent for mine."

"But do you not think, my dear, that such a termination of it all might be painful for his lordship? He did seem, only a few days ago, to be so very much in love with you."

"Painful to him? I wish I could plague him in such a way, Mrs. Stedworth! But we must not amuse ourselves in this way, at least until I really know which of his lordship's two lies is the real one. Will you set off directly, my dear, good Stedworth? You must not lose a moment. Trust me, everything will depend on the promptness, as well as the boldness, of our measures."

Mrs. Stedworth nodded. "Trust in me, my dear, that no grass shall grow under my feet or cab horse before I bring you back such a yes or no. You may depend upon it."

Mrs. Stedworth left the room, and in a few minutes, Amelia had the satisfaction of seeing her climb into a cab, driving off towards Piccadilly at full gallop.

The day was considerably advanced when Mrs. Stedworth reappeared in the drawing room. She looked so weary and exhausted that it was impossible to doubt her having made all the haste she could.

Amelia felt a great deal of anxiety to hear the first word her messenger should utter. So evenly had she contrived to balance her wishes between married, or not married, that not even Mrs. Stedworth's air of melancholy could shake her equanimity.

"What would become of me, my dear," said Mrs. Stedworth, "had I not heard you say you were prepared either way before I went out? It is dreadful to think of the wickedness of men! As sure as you sit there, my dear, you are no more Lady William Hammond that I am."

"Villain!" exclaimed Amelia. "Tell me how the matter stands at once!"

"I will, my dear. I will," Mrs. Steadworth sighed. "The church to which you went to be married is under repair. His lordship got hold of two workmen, who not only agreed to act as parson and clerk, but also got a clergyman's dress, and book, and all. As to his friend Morrison, the rascal is his own servant. This was the way, my dear child, in which we were both fooled. What a deep creature he must be, mustn't he?"

"Deep?" repeated an indignant Amelia. "He will be deep enough if all this is true. But the banns, Stedworth? Had he really the audacity to have the banns published?"

"God bless you, my dear, no. The whole business, from beginning to end, was humbug and nothing else."

Amelia ground her teeth, but recovered herself. "I shall have a letter or two to write, Mrs. Stedworth. I wish you would let the maid bring me up something by way of dinner immediately."

"I shall be very happy to wait upon you myself, Miss Thorwold!"

Amelia flinched at this name.

"I beg your pardon a thousand times, my dear young lady," said Mrs. Stedworth. "You have been defrauded of another name, and it is surely best to accustom yourself to this one again. You will soon have another, God willing."

It was not Mrs. Stedworth, however, but a sufficiently dirty charwoman who brought up Amelia's blackened chicken. It was very odd, for she had certainly never seen a chicken look so burnt during the time she had been in the house. Amelia wondered if it was an accident, or because she was no longer Lady William Hammond. The doubt did not improve her appetite, but did increase the haste in which she wrote her letters.

 

> *My dearest Mrs. Dermont,*
>
> *You will, no doubt, have seen by the papers that my poor friend, Caroline Marchmont, is no more. The few weeks I passed with her in Nice were extremely painful, but I can never cease to rejoice that I was with her to the very last. The Marchmont family have gone to Italy and kindly wished me to accompany them. But, my heart is in dear, domestic, happy England—and to England I am determined to return.*
>
> *Now, my dear and kind Mrs. Dermont, I am going to open my heart to you as I would a mother. I am quite sure you will not betray me. When the news of my poor friend's illness reached me at Crosby, I instantly decided to go to her. On mentioning my intention to my dear friend, Mrs. Knight, she laughed. Yes, kind as I have ever found her, she made light of the agony from which I was suffering. I am now quite certain she only meant to spare me the journey and sadness of witnessing the demise of my dear friend. But, at that moment, my heart rebelled against what appeared to be a great want of feeling. I left her house without*

*taking leave of her. Under these circumstances, my dear Mrs.*
*Dermont, I cannot volunteer a renewal of my visit to her. And yet, I*
*cannot resist the strong inclination I feel to revisit the dear*
*neighborhood of Stoke before returning to my usual home with*
*Lord and Lady Ripley. I have experienced too much kindness from*
*Mrs. Knight to doubt a short interview would set everything right*
*between us. But I cannot present myself at her door, after having*
*passed through it the last time in so very ungracious a manner.*

*May I, dear madam, ask you again to extend your*
*hospitality to me? It may appear to you as rather a singular*
*request, but where the heart speaks, the voice of ceremony and*
*etiquette is, I believe, seldom listened to. I shall eagerly await your*
*answer, and whatever it may be, I entreat you to believe me ever*
*most affectionately yours,*

    *Amelia Thorwold*

Amelia set the letter aside and began her next.

    *My dearest Mrs. Knight,*

    *I hope you have long ago forgiven me for the*
*impulsiveness which made me leave you so abruptly, as sincerely I*
*have forgiven you for the ridicule with which you treated my*
*sincere affection for my poor, lost Caroline. Of course, you must*
*know that the act of that sad tragedy is over. I remained with the*
*family until the day after the funeral, but declined their invitation*

*to accompany them to Rome. I might have been tempted, had not the sober hours of meditation convinced me that I must return to the fate which you have been so earnestly recommending me. In truth, I now dislike the idea much less than I did. The utter heartlessness of the man to whom I have so long given more thought than he was worth, has completely cured me of that fancy. I now see him as he really is.*

*I have written to good Mrs. Dermont, mentioning my little fracas with you, and asking permission to come to the Mount until such a time as we should have met and made it up. I hope I shall receive an agreeable answer from her, and, if so, I think all will go well. You must not be startled at seeing me in deep mourning. I could not well avoid it. Adieu, my dear friend! In the hope of soon meeting more pleasantly then we parted, I remain ever affectionately yours,*

*Amelia Thorwold*

The delight of Mrs. Dermont at receiving the letter addressed to her by the beautiful idol of her son's affections was great. Never in her whole life, perhaps, had she felt more completely happy than when she set off with it in her hand to seek him out in the shrubbery. She found him on the same bench which he had been sitting, with Julia standing in front of him, some short three months before. The good lady could not help thinking what a wonderful change had been wrought among them all. Smiling pleasantly, she walked towards them with the open letter in her hand.

"What are you thinking of, Alfred?" she asked. "Or rather, who are you thinking of, my darling son? Shall I guess, Alfred?"

He looked to his mother with a pained expression. "It is no theme for jesting, mother! What have you got there?"

"Take it, my dear," she replied, placing the letter in his hands. "When you have read it, tell me what answer you think would be most proper to give."

Alfred devoured the letter with his eyes. "She is coming back!" he said. "We must go to the house this moment. You too, Julia! You must read this divine letter to know how supremely happy I am, and not for the wealth of the worlds would I lose sight of it!"

"Then I perceive I am to say yes, Alfred? Is that it?" his mother teased.

"Unless Julia thinks we can say anything more to the purpose," he replied.

The three went back to the house together and the colonel was sent for. His consent to inviting Miss Thorwold was joyfully given, and the letter dispatched within the hour.

# Chapter 18

Miss Thorwold returned to the Mount under exactly the impression she had desired to cast, and one which she now heartily assumed.

To Alfred, she appeared an angel in mourning, coming to seek consolation in the tenderness of devoted love. To his parents, she seemed a most beautiful, caring young lady who had given touching proof that she loved their son. Even Mrs. Knight was convinced she had done her wrong in suspecting the sincerity she had professed for her dying friend. She perfectly believed that she had been to Nice and watched over Caroline's last moments, though she was a little surprised at her having spent her uncle's fifty pound gift on the trip.

It was important to Miss Thorwold that she should be married immediately, and the impatient Alfred needed no coaxing.

"Let us be married tomorrow, sweetest," he said, bending upon his knee before Amelia.

Miss Thorwold cast a smile that left no doubt in the young lover's mind that she also wished for the immediate solemnization of the ceremony.

"My dear love," Mrs. Dermont interjected, "what will our dear Amelia do about her wedding clothes? She cannot be married in mourning, dearest, can she?"

"Nobody cares so little for dress than I do," said Amelia. "When my heart is concerned I think of nothing else."

"Oh, let her wear the same gown that I first saw her in!" Alfred said. "And then let her give it to me to keep forever. And when I die, let it lie upon my bosom and be buried with me!"

The colonel laughed. "To be sure they are as deeply in love as ever two young creatures were. But I must remind you all, Lord Ripley is not likely to approve his niece being married without settlements. You all know that his consent to the marriage has been given in the handsomest manner possible, but that was when I proposed a proper settlement by a rent charge on the estate. I can't say I should like to write him again purporting that there will be no settlement because there was no time for it. I don't think it would be pleasant to do that, do you Alfred?"

"Could not the settlements be signed afterward, sir?" Alfred asked.

The colonel assumed a grave air. "Are you aware, my dear Alfred, that God forbid you should die between the time of your marriage, and at which time these parchments can be made ready, this lady would be left totally unprovided for? Are you aware of this?"

"No, I certainly am not," replied Alfred. "Neither can I be made aware of it now, father. Would not Amelia be left in your hands? And can I then have any fear of her being kindly treated?"

"I thank you, my son, for your confidence in me," replied the colonel with no less gravity. "But, believe me, on such a point it is your duty to trust no man."

His tone effectually sobered Alfred, and he remained silent.

Amelia rose from her chair and gently approached the colonel, resting her hand on his shoulder. "My dear, dear colonel, please. Please, do not for my sake let there be a moment of misunderstanding between you and my dear Alfred. Forgive his opposition, and let me make peace between you two by coaxing him to withdraw it."

She then playfully glided towards her affianced and bent her head upon his shoulder. "Dearest Alfred, say no more about it. Your dear father means nothing but kindness to us both. And besides, you ought to remember there is a great difference between waiting until you are of age, which would not be for six dismal long months, and only taking patience until the lawyers have finished the business. Were I you, I would not sit looking so unhappy about it."

Alfred, the colonel, and Mrs. Dermont all looked at her with admiration, the elegant daughter performing the part of peacemaker.

Julia Drummond had missed the interlude, preferring instead to take a tolerably long walk. She was at no great loss in which direction to turn her steps, for there was hardly a decent cottage in Stoke where she was not a familiar visitor. She stopped at the lane of a pretty little cottage on the colonel's property that was inhabited by a bold forester, a laborer of the Dermont's. She passed the lane and at the end of it, the first object to meet her eye was her old friend Susan Jenkins, who had only recently returned from work in London. The poor girl, only two years older than Julia, looked neat, but was pale, thin, and sadly out of spirits.

They warmly greeted each other, Susan unable to hide her astonishment at the growth and appearance of the young lady. Susan sat on the large, smooth stump of an old tree trunk and motioned Julia to sit beside her.

"Susan," Julia started, "I should like to return some of the fine compliments you have made to me, but I really cannot. You don't look well at all. What is the matter with you?"

"Nothing that I know of is the matter with me in the way of health, Miss Julia. If I look ill, it is only because I have been fretting. Oh, Miss Julia, I am so afraid that father and mother blame me for leaving my place and coming straight home again, without waiting in that wicked London any longer to look for a new one. I would rather earn a living by working in the fields, Miss Julia, than remain there to see and hear what I have seen and heard."

"But surely, Susan, if you have been unlucky enough to fall into the company of bad people, your parents cannot blame you for coming away?"

"They don't blame me, Miss Julia, for leaving the bad people. They just have neither room nor meat to spare."

"There does seem to be sense in their concern for that," Julia replied gently. "Did you have some particular reason for wanting to leave London altogether?"

"I had no other reason but the hating of it," she conceded. "I just thought, as you are so very near the time of being seventeen, Miss Julia, and since we have always been on good terms—"

Julia colored, but smiled at her old friend. "You remembered, Susan? My birthday is in November, and we have got to the middle of October already."

"I remember, Miss Julia. Do you think you might take me on? I mean to say, with your coming of age, would you take a maid to tend upon you? I have so little practice as I haven't been a lady's maid yet, but do have a little. The place I came from last, for the matter of a week or two, I was the only maid to a beautiful lady that lodged there. I had to wait upon her again and again. I admit when I was brushing her long hair, I used to please myself by thinking that it was good practice for me against coming to wait upon you."

Julia laughed. "Oh, if that were all the difficulty, Susan, I dare say we should get on very well! My guardian has never said a word to me about having a maid of my own. I can't be completely certain they would say yes, but I don't see them saying no, either. I hope, Susan, that your mother is not terribly angry with you for coming home, is she?"

"Oh no, Miss Julia. Mother and father are both too kind for that. But they do seem to think I was in too great a hurry, but I was not. I only wish I had not stayed quite so long, for I hate to think of such wickedness."

"Was the beautiful young lady you waited upon so wicked, Susan?"

"She was not a young lady all the time," Susan replied. "She was married while I was in the house."

"But was she wicked?" Julia asked again.

"No, Miss Julia. I did not like her very much because she was cross and fretful, and hard to please. But I don't know anything very bad of her, and if I'm not greatly mistaken, she has been sadly deceived already by them. But please, you must not ask me to talk about these dreadful people, for you are not fit to hear it. If I can come live with you, Miss Julia, I shall forget it all! I can grow again to be as innocent a girl as I ever was. Will you be so very kind as to ask the colonel about it, Miss Julia?"

"You may depend upon it, my dear Susan. You shall hear from me as soon as I have got his answer."

On entering the drawing room Julia found Miss Thorwold surrounded by the colonel, his lady, and Alfred. She was sitting near a writing table with an open note in her hand.

"Here is our dear Julia!" exclaimed Alfred. "She must help me persuade you, my Amelia, not to commit the cruelty of running away from us at a moment when your presence is so necessary. I cannot bear patiently the tortured delay of the lawyers without you. Mrs. Knight wants to take her away from us, Julia! Tell her that it is her duty to stay."

Amelia had, immediately on her return to the Mount, apologized in the most penitent style to Julia. This apology, and all the coaxing series of civilities that followed, increased Julia's inexplicit distrust of Amelia. Unfortunately, there was no help for it. She had to submit to a vast deal of seeming affection, which greatly added to the sum of her daily suffering.

"Let me state the case," said Miss Thorwold. She playfully pressed a stick of sealing wax upon the lips of Alfred, in token that he was not to speak. "I will not allow our dear Julia to be prejudiced. Here is a letter from Mrs. Knight, Miss Drummond, inviting me to return to Crosby. Ought I refuse or accept it?"

"We cannot but suppose, Miss Thorwold, that your friend, Mrs. Knight, would be the first to insist on you declining her request if she knew that you could *only* be removed from the Mount by the stern command of duty."

"Oh, how well you know her, my dear Julia! She would indeed! I was determined that you should decide the point, and you have done it. Now, for my answer—I shall no longer find it difficult. I will go to her for a week or two as a matter of politeness, and return to the Mount directly afterward."

Amelia drew the writing materials toward her and set about on the note to Mrs. Knight.

Julia had not forgotten her promise to Susan, either. While Alfred and Amelia indulged in a quiet walk through the wilderness, she opened up to both her guardian and his lady the state of affairs. She assured them she did not need a maid to wait upon her, but if she did have any maid at all, she would much rather it be Susan than anybody else.

The colonel smiled upon her with a great deal of affectionate good humor. "You are to come of age at seventeen, and there is but a week or two wanting of it now, Julia. I suppose most people would think that your having a maid for the future was rather more than was necessary, but Mrs. Dermont likes it as well as I, in order that you may at once feel the comfort of being a young lady in her majority. You have my leave, and Mrs. Dermont's leave too, my dear, to tell Susan Jenkins she may hold herself engaged to come into the house on the 15th of next month."

Julia thanked them both for their kindness and set off on another solitary walk to carry the good news to Susan.

# Chapter 19

Miss Thorwold left to enjoy the hospitality of her good friend, Mrs. Knight, and soon after, the morning arrived to which the colonel had been looking forward to for years. He had never said a word to Julia or Alfred of the manner in which every sixpence of Julia's income had been hoarded, in order to augment her little fortune. He had frequently mentioned that the fortune bequeathed to her was seven thousand pounds, but never gave the slightest hint that it had been increased by more than half solely by his good management.

At breakfast, the colonel set the example of wishing her joy. As soon as the meal was over he addressed her with a happy look, but said with an equal degree of solemnity, "My dear Julia, I must request the favor of your company in my library."

Julia immediately got up to attend to him.

"I should wish you, Alfred, to come too," he added, "and your mother also, if she so wishes."

The large table that stood in the center of the room was covered with papers. A large parchment of several sheets was laid wide open.

"Have the kindness to sit down, all of you," said the colonel.

He drew a multitude of accounts toward him and read aloud the sums he had been receiving from Julia's income over the years, which he replaced entirely in her name with regularity.

"And now, my dear," he concluded, placing the printed documents in her hand, "I have the pleasure of presenting you with vouchers which prove you to be in the possession of stock. It is worth exactly ten thousand seven hundred pounds sterling. Will you give me a kiss for having managed your little money matters so well?"

Julia hastened to him and granted the requested kiss. "You must forgive my being so very stupid, my dear sir, but how can I have more than ten thousand pounds when only seven thousand were left to me?"

This question was exactly what the colonel had been looking forward to answering for the last fifteen years. "I defrayed all your expenses, my dear. I endeavored, in all things, to treat you as a daughter, in order to prove how constantly I kept in mind the service rendered to me by your gallant grandfather."

Julia returned her thanks for all his kindness in a simple, unmistakably sincere manner.

"Now then, my young lady, you may consider yourself the most independent person in the family. You have only to write a line to our broker and good friend, Mr. Wood, telling him to send you a power of attorney by post. When you have signed it, you may give it to anybody you please, who may straight away sell as much stock as you choose to order, out the funds and change it all into half crowns."

"Thank you, sir," replied Julia. "I shall remember your instructions if ever I am seized with a longing for amusement."

"Without troubling Mr. Wood at all, here is enough to amuse yourself, I hope, for six months to come. Here, my dear," he continued, spreading a number of notes on the table, "here is the first dividend upon your property that I have ever drawn out of the bank. I received this last July and, unless you follow my instructions and send to the broker, you won't have anymore until January. Here, my child. Put it up and take care of it, like a good girl."

Julia looked half frightened at the notes. "Is it possible that all of this is mine?"

"All this, my dear?" asked the colonel, shaking his head. "It is all very well for the purchase of bobbins and bows, and to pay the wages of your own maid, you know. As long as I live you won't want for anything else. But, in case no more Honorable Mr. Borrowdales should happen to come your way, I fear you may find that it is but a poor income after all. However, I have a scheme in my head that will bring it up, without the slightest danger, to above five hundred pounds. I have heard of a capital good mortgage, Julia, and you must sell out of the funds, my dear. You must invest your money in that. I am expecting in almost every post to learn the last particulars about it, and then, the thing shall be settled at once. When this is done I shall feel more at ease about you."

The remainder of this important day was passed, for the most part, in conversation between Alfred and his parents upon the probable duration of Amelia's visit to Mrs. Knight. The earliest possible day on which they might hope to hear that the settlements were completed was a equally popular topic.

"If Miss Thorwold does not return to The Mount quickly, I shall go over to Crosby and take possession of her myself," declared Alfred.

Mrs. Dermont suggested it might be as well to write a pleading letter to Mrs. Knight. In the name of love and pity, Alfred might beseech her to remit a few days of the time she'd stipulated. This measure was acted upon, a letter cordially written, and delivered to Mrs. Knight at her breakfast table.

The lady of Crosby perused the letter with a satirical smile, and then handed it to her friend.

Miss Thorwold read the dispatch and laid it down quietly, returning to her coffee and roll. "I must go."

"Must go, Amelia? Upon my word, my dear, I think you are beginning your obedience rather too early. Why must you go?"

"Because I do not like to run the risk of displeasing any of them. It is quite as well to keep things going smoothly, you know."

Mrs. Knight looked at her steadily for a moment. "As I live, Amelia, I do believe that beautiful creature Alfred has touched your fancy at last. Do not be ashamed to confess it. You really need not."

Miss Thorwold looked at her and smiled. "My dear Mrs. Knight, I am simply endeavoring to settle my mind quietly on the fate that is before me. Please, for the future, talk no more to me about the state of my heart."

"Very true, my dear. You are quite right and I am quite wrong. So, if you really have any heart left we will endeavor to forget it."

"Thank you," returned Amelia. "Perhaps you had better answer the Dermont dispatch."

"Oh! True! I forgot the man was waiting. But I hope that you do not really mean to run away from me yet?"

"You are excessively kind, Mrs. Knight, but I am sure you must feel as I do. I have made up my mind to form this connection and make all things smooth between us while preparing for it. I really do beg you to tell them in your answer that I shall be ready to attend to them when they come for me."

Mrs. Knight uttered not a single word in reply. She drew towards her a little writing table and wrote the answer as nearly as possible in the terms dictated. She lit her taper, slid the note into its cover, sealed it, rang the bell, and gave it to the servant without indicating by word or look whether she approved or not.

The manner in which the dispatch was received at the Mount was entirely different from this profound silence.

Mrs. Dermont clasped her hands and lifted her eyes to heaven. "Was there ever such a dear, gentle, affectionate creature as our sweet Amelia? Ah, Alfred! It is quite plain that you may lead her anyway you wish, but I hope it will always be by a silken rein!"

Julia heard the note read out loud and quietly slipped from the room, determined upon a long, solitary walk. She took the path across the fields which led to the Grange. She did not contemplate walking there when she set out, but by the time she had fully made up her mind to visit Charlotte Verepoint, she discovered to her considerable surprise that she was within ten minutes walk of the house.

She found both Mrs. and Miss Verepoint most cordially glad to see her, though a good deal surprised at her mode of arrival.

"I am quite delighted to find that the Mount is within a walk, Julia," said Miss Verepoint. "You do not intend to walk back again, do you?"

"Oh, yes I do!" replied Julia. "I do not feel the least fatigued, though I confess I got here without knowing at all what I was about. I certainly think that Mrs. Dermont would have believed my premature coming of age had led to insanity if I had told her of such an excursion."

"And she might well think, my dear, that I was in the same condition if I allowed you to return on foot," said Mrs. Verepoint.

"Why should she return home at all?" asked Charlotte. "Stay here, Miss Drummond. We have been meaning to invite you since Mrs. Dermont so kindly hosted a stay of my own. Mother and I were only just discussing it recently!"

"Upon my word, I think that is just the thing!" said the old lady. "What cause have you to show, my dear, why we should not keep you, now that we have got possession?"

"None in the world, my dear Mrs. Verepoint," Julia replied. "Only, I don't exactly see how I am to dress for dinner."

"And what is a new maid for if she cannot pack up her lady's dresses?" asked Charlotte.

Julia blushed at hearing others knew she was to have a maid. "She—Susan—hasn't yet started in my employ."

"If you will please write your orders to your maid, Susan, I will undertake to send them. By far the best way will be to send the carriage over for both the maid and the wardrobe."

Julia sat down without making any further objections and wrote to Mrs. Dermont. She relayed the fact of her having come upon the Grange without being aware she was so near it, and all the consequences which had followed upon her mistaking the distance so pleasantly. The reply came soon after. It not only expressed Mrs. Dermont's satisfaction at knowing her dear Julia was to enjoy a visit with Mrs. and Miss Verepoint, but rejoiced that she should have timed it so well. The approaching arrival of their Amelia would prevent her from feeling the loss of her society, as they must have done at any other time.

# Chapter 20

At the Mount, everything went on most happily. Julia, not quite forgotten, was certainly not much thought of by anyone. The first two days after Amelia's return were joyful for Alfred, who seemed to be living at her feet.

The beautiful source of all this happiness was momentarily interrupted by the arrival of a letter for Miss Thorwold. Had the letter been fastened by a wafer, Amelia would have been immediately put on guard and opened it privately. It was instead sealed with a good impression of a true-lover's knot, a symbol in no way alarming. She opened it and read the first few lines, which sufficed to make her turn as pale as a ghost. Alfred flew to her side, and placing one hand around her waist, seized the cold, damp fingers which held the fatal letter. Amelia quietly withdrew her hand and allowed her head to sink upon his chest.

"Oh, dearest Alfred, I feel very ill. Take me to the window. I need air!"

The young man clasped her in his arms and helped her across the room. The colonel hastened to Alfred's assistance, throwing up the sash and opening the window. Amelia exchanged the letter with a handkerchief in her pocket, and pressed the cloth against her brow.

Mrs. Dermont rushed to Amelia with a bottle of pungent salts. She was about to apply them under the nose of her patient, when her hand was gently pushed aside. "Thank you a thousand times, my dear Mrs. Dermont, but the feeling of faintness has entirely passed away. I am quite well now. I am sadly afraid I have frightened you all."

"You have received some bad news I fear, my dear child," said the colonel, looking at her tenderly.

"Oh no!" she replied, almost laughing. "I certainly do not wonder at your thinking so. I felt like fainting, but can easily account for it. Do you remember how I walked last night with Alfred on the terrace? We were both of us so deeply occupied by looking at the moon, that I quite forgot how late it was. I confess now that I did not sleep well, and a feeling of fatigue has hung about me all morning. You must take better care of me, Alfred, in future."

Alfred's features were overcome with regretful compassion. "My dear, would you like to lie down quietly in the library while I read to you?"

Amelia nodded her head yes and permitted the worried Alfred to install her on a sofa in the library, placing himself in a low armchair beside it. As Alfred was about to open a book of poems, Amelia gently took his hand.

"I must yield my weakness to you, Alfred, for at this moment your strength is necessary."

"What is it, my dear Amelia? Tell me how I can help you?"

"Listen to me with your best and coolest judgment, for only you can help me, if, indeed, help is still possible. That letter, Alfred, is from a London lawyer. It threatens me with instant arrest if I do not immediately find the means of paying into his hands the sum of thirteen hundred pounds."

Alfred colored slightly, looking dismayed. "Why has the impertinent fellow not sent it to your uncle, instead of audaciously intruding himself upon you here, my sweet love? How was this claim contracted, Amelia?"

"Therein, my dearest, lies the difficulty," she replied. "The large amount will at once show you that it is not likely to be for any expense of my own. If it was possible there would be no difficulty in the business whatsoever, after scolding me a little for my extravagance, perhaps, would my uncle pay it instantly. But, most unhappily, the debt has been incurred by one whose name cannot be mentioned in connection with Lord Ripley."

"Then how, dearest, have you been led to become responsible for the debts of a person so detached from your uncle?"

"Ah, there is the rub, Alfred. This is the point on which I wish to open my heart to you. Lord Ripley, as you well know, has one legitimate child, the Honorable Mr. Thorwold, his son and heir. But he also has, though few know anything about it, a natural daughter, several years older than his son. When my mother, who survived my poor father by only a few years, died, I was taken into my uncle's house. It has been my home ever since. His establishment consists of two houses. One is in London and the other is in Cornwall. Lord Ripley was passionately fond of his country home and would pass the summer months there. Lady Ripley is no aunt of mine, and as nothing belonging to her lord is particularly dear to her, she never felt any affection for me. As a consequence, I was more at the country house than the one in town. While in Cornwall I formed a strong attachment to the natural daughter of my uncle, who certainly was very strongly attached to me also. She resided permanently at her father's house there and made my life one of unceasing joy. She had been most carefully educated and was never so happy as when instructing me. This happy intercourse continued until I was eighteen, and then she married. It is needless for me to go into the details of this unhappy marriage. It is enough to say that the man turned out to be little more than a swindler. Unfortunately, his poor wife was devotedly attached to him and never would believe he was unworthy. Her continued adherence to him so irritated her father, that it ended with a quarrel, and they never made up. Her misery over this and all her other misfortunes was more than her health could bear. She fell into a lingering decline which only terminated in her death, and it was during her last illness that this terrible debt was contracted. Her worthless husband had been arrested and dragged to prison, and it was her agony under this that induced me to put my name on the bill upon which this claim is founded. Now, Alfred, you know all."

The look on Alfred's face was all Miss Thorwold needed to confirm her performance was a success. He practically swooned before her. "All this, my dearest love, only adds to my devoted, idolizing affection of you! But why, my beloved, should you allow this to alarm your spirits so severely? I cannot doubt that a single word from you to Lord Ripley would induce him to release you from it instantly. You have only to sit down and write to him, dearest Amelia, and the disagreeable business will be over. One word will suffice."

"Yes, Alfred," replied Miss Thorwold in despair, "one word would suffice to make him throw me from him forever as he did his daughter before. Alfred, you do not know him! Lord Ripley has many high and noble qualities, but he long ago told me if I continued to speak to his daughter after he cut her off, he would never see or talk to me again."

Alfred looked distressed. "If this is so, my dear Amelia, you must of course apply to my father. I can easily imagine, dearest, that doing so would be disagreeable to you. But I see no alternative."

"Then Alfred," she replied, "I must prepare my mind for the worst. I must go to prison."

"Go to prison, Amelia, instead of throwing yourself upon the kindness of my excellent father? I cannot, I will not, I do not believe it!"

"Most sad will be the task of convincing you, dearest, that you are mistaken."

Alfred offered the tenderest smile. "Not only sad, but impossible, my love. I understand you now, my sweet Amelia! You shrink, dearest, from the task of repeating that sad story to him. I must do it for you."

Amelia rose suddenly from the sofa, her countenance one of great agony. "Gracious heaven! Would you betray me? Have I trusted you for this? Have I opened my breaking heart before your eyes only to be rewarded with you threatening to disclose to your father my secret?"

"You must not put my generous father in the same light as your uncle, Amelia. If you will only consent to go upstairs and lie down for half an hour, I will promise to resolve this whole affair to your satisfaction. Will you let me manage it?"

"No, sir, I will not," said Amelia severely. "I have confided in you with all the trust of perfect love! Now you threaten me with the repetition of my dreadful tale to the last individual in the world who I would ever wish it disclosed to? You have my secret, sir. I cannot recall the words I have told you, but I will not see you again. My resolution is taken. I shall submit myself without struggle to the power of the law. Your father's house shall not be disgraced by me."

He took her hand and gently sat her back on the sofa, falling upon his knees before her. "Tell me, my dearest, sweetest love. Tell me now what you think would be best for me to do, and I will do it!"

She impressed a kiss on his forehead. "You must forgive me, Alfred. The shock of this letter has overtaken me. Your affection, your true sympathy, has restored me to myself. I now feel able to consult with you on what will be best to do. You still, I think, are just a month or two from being of age, dear Alfred?"

"Five months," he replied. "Beyond the allowance my father gives me, I have nothing. This allowance is to be supplemented with half of his entire income when we marry, but I should fear that paying this sum in less than three or four years, my sweet love, might require a degree of economy which would interfere with your comfort."

"And with yours too, dearest Alfred. I should be miserable to witness any discomfort of your part. As it is evident that the money must be paid directly, it must be borrowed, Alfred. My dear heart tells me, dear love, that you could secure a loan against your future income easily. My fate is sealed unless you can apply to a friend who would feel your word to be worth more than your bond. A true and real friend who knows you well, Alfred. Have you such a friend?"

"There are several who would trust me, my dear Amelia, but none who would have such a sum to lend."

She knit her brows. "Julia Drummond has no money, Alfred?"

Alfred colored violently. "Julia Drummond? I could not take money from her."

"Then let us quit the subject, Mr. Dermont. For me to know that you have the power to save me and decline to do it is, after all, the most effectual way of enabling me to say goodbye to you forever."

"Amelia!" he exclaimed. "Spare me, I beseech you, from hearing of you talk of our parting! It is not possible, Amelia! It is not possible to lose you and live. There is nothing you can ask which I will not be ready to do. Let me hear you promise to be mine forever, and I will do anything you ask!"

"Go to her, Alfred. Address Miss Drummond carefully with a petition that she might lend you, for a few years, on interest, the sum of thirteen hundred pounds. Should she have the childish indiscretion of asking what the money is for, tell her the time will probably come when you no longer wish to conceal it from her, but at present it cannot be disclosed. Guard from her the true purpose and the name of the woman you mean to make your wife. She will keep it a secret from all, dear Alfred, I know it! Will you do this? Will you, for the love of me?"

He instantly and solemnly replied, "Amelia, I will."

Amelia watched as he went. She watched the door close after him, she listened to his rapidly departing steps in the hall, and then quietly turned to a looking glass. "Should I have known how speedily I might settle the accounts, I most certainly would have indulged in one or two more gowns," she said to herself.

# Chapter 21

Luckily for Alfred, the ride to the Grange was a short one. It was not his object to be shown into Mrs. Verepoint's drawing room, as this would've necessitated asking Julia to accompany him elsewhere. Instead, he told the servant that he wished to see Miss Drummond for a moment, and would be much obliged if she would come down to him.

The man replied by opening the door of the library, and there stood Julia, busily engaged in seeking the volume she wanted.

"This is a piece of good luck, Julia," he said. "I wanted to see you for five minutes alone."

Julia smiled at her dear friend. "I'm happy to see you, Alfred. Have you come to tell me something?"

He let out a heavy sigh. "Tell you, Julia? No, I did not come to tell you anything. I confess, I came to perform a difficult task. I come to ask a favor of you."

"I do not think it could be anything but a pleasure for me to grant anything you ask, Alfred."

"God bless you, my dear and ever kind Julia. I know I am a fool for dreading to ask a friend who is in every way indulgent, but I am. I come to ask you to lend me some money."

Julia's face lit up in delight. "Lend you money, my dearest Alfred? How very glad I am to hear it! I have at this moment more money in my writing desk at home than I have any idea what to do with. You may take it all, and are welcome. Here is the key to the desk," she said, disengaging a key fastened to her watch chain. "Please hold onto the key until I come home again. I really never thought that having money could give me so much pleasure."

Alfred turned scarlet. "My dear, dear Julia! It is painfully embarrassing for me to tell you that no sum you could have in your desk could be sufficient for what I want. Julia, I have immediate need, a most urgent need, of thirteen hundred pounds."

It was now Julia's turn to color. "Oh Alfred, what a fool I am! I know absolutely nothing about money. A very little seems to me enough for everything. I really am quite ashamed of myself, as if it would be worth your while to ask for what my guardian gave me for my wants and wishes. Thank goodness there is no time lost by my blundering, for you have only to give my love to the colonel and tell him that you can have exactly what you want, the quick way he told me, without losing a post."

"My father can no longer regulate the disposal of your money, Julia," Alfred replied, his voice faltering. "You are now of age, it is only your own signature that can avail."

"But what am I to sign, Alfred?—Oh! I remember now about the power of attorney. How in the world can I manage to get such a thing? Gallop home as fast as you can and ask your father to write to old Mr. Wood. He may send me the letter if it is proper for me to sign it. Or, I can walk home across the fields and sign it there, if you think that would be quickest. Shall I set off directly, Alfred?"

"No, Julia," he said. "It is not only yourself who must sign the letter to the broker, but you must also write it. In short, my dearest Julia, my father must never know."

The bright glow of affectionate pleasure faded instantly. "Oh, Alfred! He is so very, very kind and he loves you so dearly! Think better of it, my dearest Alfred. Think how it is impossible that he could be angry with you. Do you not feel that it is impossible?"

"Julia," he begged, "spare me from having to explain all this to you. I am not so much to blame as you think me. I have no power, no right—"

Julia held up her hand. "Of course, Alfred. I do not mean to dictate to you. Just tell me the words to write and it shall be done directly."

Had Alfred been aware how perfectly certain Julia felt that he was borrowing her money for Miss Thorwold, he would not have been able to honestly assure Amelia, upon his return, that he had managed the affair successfully. But she accepted his words and manner, clapping her triumphant hands and thanking him sincerely when he delivered the news.

The next morning, after the conclusion of the borrowing and paying transaction, a large, brown paper parcel arrived by mail. It was directed to Colonel Dermont and upon being opened was found to contain the impatiently awaited settlements, all fairly engrossed and ready for signing. Alfred saw them, seized upon them, and held them in his delighted grasp.

All now was a joyous bustle of confusion at the Mount. Measures had long ago been taken for the immediate solemnization of the marriage. Excepting the actual preparing of the wedding banquet and announcing to the guests the date, little remained to be done. The marriage of Colonel Dermont's heir, however, was not an event to be done in private. As many distant guests as could be comfortably accommodated for this great and joyful occasion were to be lodged in rooms at the Mount. Near neighbors offered additional rooms in their own houses for those who could not. Mrs. Knight was the first to volunteer her home and services. Mrs. Verepoint thoughtfully suggested that Miss Drummond's room might prove useful to the Dermonts, and urged Julia to remain at the Grange until the wedding party had dispersed. No one at the Mount made any objection to it, and the matter was speedily settled.

The finest breakfast was in preparation. Grapes and pines were to be as plenty as gooseberries and currants at a summer fair. Grouse was to fly to them with railroad speed from Scotland, and every covert in the county held itself honored to contribute its contingent of pheasants and partridges.

The day after the arrival of the marriage settlements, another dispatch from his lawyer was delivered to Colonel Dermont at the breakfast table. The perusal of the documents appeared to give him much satisfaction.

"Any commands for the Grange, Mrs. Dermont?" he asked. "I am going to ride over immediately after breakfast."

"Yes indeed, colonel, I have a command," replied Mrs. Dermont. "You must be sure to see Julia, if you please, and tell her that she must send me over Susan directly. She has not been very long used to her services, you know, so I don't suppose Julia will miss her much for the next day or two."

Julia was the only person he wished to see on a matter of real business, and on arrival he only asked for her.

"Both young ladies are in the garden, colonel," answered the man.

"Then go there after them, Richard. Tell Miss Drummond that I wish to speak to her for five minutes in the library."

The message was delivered and the summons obeyed, and the colonel proved himself to be a trusty messenger in executing his lady's errand.

"I shall be delighted if she can be useful," said Julia. "I will go and send her off directly, sir, if you will give me leave."

"Do so, my dear, and then our consciences will be at rest in that matter. But come back to me as soon as you can."

Within minutes Julia returned and stated that Susan was on her way.

"Now, Julia, I am going to prove to you that coming of age is really a serious affair, when the possession of money comes with it. It will be necessary that you listen very carefully, in order that you should understand what I have to say."

She answered with a smile.

"You remember, I hope, all I said about my being sorry that the interest you earned was so small. I had hoped I might be able to put you in the way of making it better. Do you remember all this, my dear?"

"Yes sir," replied Julia. "Yes sir, I do."

"Well then, my dear, what I have come to tell you is that my good friend Wright has managed the business admirably for us. He has got a mortgage with a security as firm as a freehold can make it. It will make a great difference in your income. The difficulty is that the sum needed is eleven thousand, and you have only ten thousand seven hundred, but I am willing and able to lend you the difference. All you have now to do is sign this power of attorney and I will forward it to Mr. Wood, the broker, who will place the money into the hands of Mr. Wright. Here is a pen and ink, Julia—and here is where you are to put your name."

"I fear you will be very angry with me, Colonel Dermont, but I am no longer in possession of the sum you made over to me. I have already spent thirteen hundred pounds."

"Spent thirteen hundred pounds in less than three weeks, Miss Julia Drummond?" he cried. "You really must excuse me, young lady, if I confess that I don't believe a word of it. You are either making a joke, you foolish child, or else you have some very dangerous notion in your thoughts about keeping ready money in your own hands. Tell me the truth at once, Julia."

"The truth will, I well know, make you very angry, dear sir. I have lent the money to a friend and have pledged not to disclose the transaction to you."

"Not disclose the transaction to me!" repeated the colonel. "And who can the precious scoundrel be who made this condition with you? And do you not in your head, Julia, see that this condition alone stamps your friend as a villain? Answer this question honestly, Julia—does this desire to separate you from the protection of the only protector you have in the world, does it not prove him to be a villain?"

"Oh, no sir!" replied Julia, bursting into tears. "No, sir, no! He is not a villain!"

Colonel Dermont looked earnestly in her face for a moment, then sighed deeply. "This mystery most unhappily clears up another. I now understand why you refused Mr. Borrowdale. It is but too plain that, young as you are, your affections have been seduced by some unworthy wretch, one who dares not avow himself to your friends. He made you give away your property and tell you his name cannot be mentioned? For your own sake, Julia, stop this now. You are on the high road to destruction, and though your grandfather saved my life, you won't let me do anything to save you."

The colonel's eyes filled with tears and revealed much more sorrow than anger. Julia cried even harder, shocked at the idea of the colonel believing she had a secret lover.

"Answer me one question, Julia. If you will I will say no more, and endeavor to settle your remaining money in some way or other that might prevent your being scandalously robbed again in the future. Only tell me, upon your honor, that the person you have lent this money is not one whom you have bestowed the affections of your heart."

Julia closed her eyes so she wouldn't have to meet the inquiring look that was fixed upon his face, her own burning with crimson. She covered it with both her hands and could not speak.

"Then it is so," he sighed. "It has been settled among us, Julia Drummond, that our dear son and his charming wife should take up their residence at the Mount. It is my first duty now to take measures to prevent the lovely, high born wife of my son from being disgraced by association with a young female who has so shamefully misconducted herself. This being the case I should wish you to accept an old lady's invitation, your mother's aunt in Scotland, who has written in the past to Mrs. Dermont for your company. We have put it off because we did not want to lose you, and Alfred, you know, was always against your going. But now I must insist. Arrangements will be made for you to leave immediately, unless you tell me this villain's name."

He laid his hand on the lock of the door. "Only tell me his name, Julia! I would rather do anything than part with you!"

Julia shook her head. "Impossible."

The door was opened and closed again, and Julia Drummond was left completely alone.

The first person the colonel met upon entering his house was Alfred, who was immediately struck by the melancholy countenance of his father. "Good heaven, my dear sir! What is the matter? You have heard some bad news, I am certain. Is it anything about Amelia? Anything to postpone our wedding day?"

The colonel rubbed his hand across his forehead. "I have learned something which grieves me to the heart, dear boy. Come to the library and I will tell you all that I know. Perhaps you might be able to give me a hint upon a subject that is a complete mystery to me."

Knowing Amelia was in the act of fitting her wedding dress and being determined not to interrupt, he followed his father without opposition.

"Alfred," said the colonel when they had both seated themselves, "I have found out one mystery but fallen upon another. I have discovered why Julia Drummond refused Mr. Borrowdale."

"Really, sir, there is no great mystery in that," replied Alfred. "She refused him because she did not like him."

"Good. But why did she not like him, Alfred?" returned the colonel. "How was it possible that any young girl could help liking him, unless she liked another better?"

"I do not think so, sir."

"It is past thinking, Alfred. As far as being attached to another man, she has confessed it, Alfred."

"I do not believe it, sir," Alfred said, crossing his arms. "You must have misunderstood her. I do not believe it for a single moment."

"My dear Alfred, you mistake me altogether. You will know exactly what was said if you will listen to me for a moment."

Colonel Dermont related the steps he had taken in order to obtain for Julia a more profitable investment for her money. He then went on to describe his interview with her, stating very fairly all that had been said on both sides.

The feelings with which Alfred listened to this narrative were decidedly the most painful he had ever experienced. The generous act of Julia, and then the greatly more generous act of her silence in the face of so degrading an accusation—in the face of banishment—for the sake of saving Amelia, was more than he could bear. He could not doubt Amelia's feelings on the subject would be the same and his, and yielded to this persuasion. He laid his hand upon the arm of his father and related the whole affair exactly as it had passed, taking care to make Amelia's part reflect shining proof of her generous, confiding temper.

The colonel went completely pale and slumped in his chair. "Reproach me, Alfred. It is impossible you can reproach me too much. That I should be such a fool at to believe that dear, innocent young creature could have picked up a vagabond of a lover, and given her money to him! I shall never forgive myself."

"Let us be thankful," said Alfred, "that no worse mischief has been done than paining her gentle heart for an hour or two. Would it tire you, sir, to ride over to the Grange again? To tell her you have heard the whole story from me? I would willingly go myself, but she certainly does deserve an apology from you."

"I will go now, my son. This very instant!"

The colonel returned to the Grange to find Julia still in the library, sitting limply beside a window.

"Julia Drummond," he said, hand over his heart, "my dear child, can you ever forgive me?"

The two sat together and the colonel recounted his conversation with Alfred, the details of Amelia's kind gesture that led to her near arrest, and the admiration felt by all in Julia so faithfully keeping her promise. Julia was just receiving a hearty farewell benediction from the colonel, when the door of Mrs. Verepoint's library was suddenly thrown open, and Susan Jenkins, struggling against the efforts of the servant preventing her entrance, rushed into the room.

# Chapter 22

The countenance of Susan Jenkins was violently flushed. She trembled from having over exerted herself walking with great speed from the Mount. She caught hold of a chair as she came into the room, sunk into it, and burst into tears.

"What is the matter, Susan?" cried Julia.

"Who is hurt? Who is ill?" asked the colonel.

Out of breath, the girl weakly replied, "Nobody is hurt or ill."

"Then she has been ill treated or hurt herself, Julia," said Colonel Dermont. He took the girl's hand in his to feel her pulse. "I think the poor girl is going to faint. She ought to have a glass of wine, or some drops, or something."

Julia made her way up the stairs with all speed to Mrs. Verepoint and gave an account of the girl's condition. Mrs. Verepoint, both alarmed and curious, hurried to the library with Julia. Charlotte was dispatched to find a glass of wine and told the servant it was not necessary to come into the room with her. A bottle of strong salts in the hands of the old lady had already proved useful, and the glass of wine brought by her daughter did even more to restore the girl's complexion. The colonel thought the best thing he could do would be to take his leave, trusting the nervous young waiting maid to the care of the kind ladies who surrounded her.

Susan saw the colonel make way for the door and sat straight up. "Pray sir, let me beg you as the very greatest favor not to go! I have got something that concerns you to tell. I did not know that I should have the good fortune of finding you here, and it was to Miss Julia that I meant to tell it all, but it is far better and more proper that it should be you, sir."

"If it is something which concerns the colonel, young woman," said Mrs. Verepoint gently, "then my daughter and I had better go. I dare say Colonel Dermont and Miss Drummond will give you leave to relax again, for you do not look yet as if you are quite able to sit erect."

"No, good madam, no," replied Susan. "I have nothing to say but what ought to be known. Yet, I would rather that both these young ladies were away. My horrid story is not fit for their ears."

The two girls needed no second hint and left the room. Susan relaxed back in the chair, yet it seemed doubtful for a minute or two, in her state of agitation, that she would be able to execute her purpose. Colonel Dermont suspected the disclosure would be of a rustic adventure the anxious young woman would want to distance herself from, but on communicating this suspicion to Mrs. Verepoint, she shook her head to show her disagreement. She saw an air of great innocence and modesty in Susan Jenkins and, though prepared to hear a tale unfit for Miss Drummond and Miss Verepoint's ears, she felt strongly the poor girl was not the heroine of it.

"Now then, young woman," said the kindly Mrs. Verepoint, "tell us at once what has affected you so strongly."

Susan paused for another moment to decide where she should begin, then said, "My last service in London was in the house of Mrs. Stedworth, on Half Moon Street, Piccadilly. I never quite liked it because there was something I could not make out in the manner in which so many fine ladies and gentlemen came to visit my mistress. She looked and talked as much like a lady as anybody when she chose to, but this was not always, and it was strange to see the great difference between the people that came to visit her. Besides letting lodgings, she made a trade of buying and selling ladies' clothes. The people who bought and the people who sold all seemed intimate with her. About two months ago, or rather more, I was ordered to set the drawing room floor for a new lady lodger. Two days later, the most beautiful young lady came. I had to wait upon her and dress her, and so, of course, I soon came to know her face quite well. Directly after she came there was a gentleman who visited her daily, dining with her most days, but never failing to come every evening. His name was Lord William, and I never heard any other name. My mistress and the young lady, whose name I never heard at all—for my mistress always called her 'drawing room' or 'the drawing room lady' when she spoke of her—but my mistress and this young lady never scrupled to talk before me. As I brushed her hair or helped her into a dress, they always spoke about her going to get married to Lord William. When at last the day came, my mistress made no secret to me about it. She said that she was going to church with them, and a hackney coach came to the door in the morning, which took Lord William, the young lady, and my mistress away. They came back about an hour later and I had, according to my orders, had breakfast laid for them all in the drawing room. After they breakfasted, I was sent to call another coach for the bride and bridegroom. I heard it ordered to some railroad station, but I forget which. At the end of a fortnight they came back again, and then Lord William lodged in the house too as the husband of the lady. For a few days they seemed just as new married people might be. During this time my mistress always called her Lady William, but it was only a little while before I began to see a change in more ways than one. Lady William seemed to grow cross and out of spirits, while my mistress grew gayer and smarter looking every day. She could manage to look very handsome too, and she used to dress as nice as any lady to go to the door when Lord William came home to dinner. He started to change his way of knocking and came to the door with a single tap, but still my mistress seemed to know it was him, for she always went to the door herself. He started to turn into the front parlor before he went upstairs, and would sit with my mistress for near upon an hour together. At last, the lord and lady had a quarrel, and my lord came downstairs into the parlor and sat there longer, I should think, than an hour before going out. My mistress came to me in the kitchen and told me to take tea up to my lady, and ask her if she wanted anything. I did, and she told me she was going to bed. Afterward my mistress told me I must go to bed too, for his lordship was not coming home and she wanted the house quiet. My bed was in a very little room on the parlor floor, just at the top of the kitchen stairs. I didn't go to bed because I had a bit of sewing to do for myself, but I sat as quiet as possible so I would not disturb anybody. About half past one in the morning a gentle tap come to the door of the house, as if it was made with fingers instead of the knocker. At first I was frightened because of the late hour and thought that if it was anybody at all, it must be a thief trying some of their London tricks to get in. Afraid of this, I pushed the bolt upon my own door and stood in all tremble to listen. I heard creeping steps in the passage and looked through the key hole, plainly seeing Lord William with my mistress. She had a candle in her hand and I saw her make signs to him to keep quiet, pointing towards my door to show that he might be heard. They remained together," said Susan, in a manner that showed her reluctance to enter upon such details, "all the night."

She looked to her fingers and would not meet the colonel or Mrs. Verepoint's eyes. "On the following morning Lord William went out before breakfast, but employed himself in the parlor for some time before he did so. He wrote a letter to the lady and gave me the letter for her as he went out. My mistress was with her when I delivered it, and something that I said in answer to a question the lady asked gave Mrs. Stedworth reason to suppose that I knew what happened the night before. She followed me out of the room calling me every sort of name, and she called the charwoman to bear witness that I was turned out as a thief, a liar, and worse. I did not try to defend myself and just got away as quickly as possible."

Susan paused and fixed her eyes upon the ground, remaining silent. She then stood up and seemed intent to say more, but her color varied and was too agitated to speak.

The colonel evidently thought the long story belonged to a class of narratives usually called *cock and bull*. He shrugged his shoulders and said, "Well, my girl, I suppose I may go now?"

Even Mrs. Verepoint thought they had been detained for a long time on very little purpose. Rather coldly, she said, "I dare say, young woman, you are very glad to have exchanged so disreputable a place for one so very different. But there is not use in talking about it now."

She rose up to attend the colonel out of the room.

Susan stretched out her hand in panic of their departure to stop their exit. In a deep, hollow, barely audible whisper she said, "That lady, and Mr. Alfred's intended wife, are the same person."

The effects produced by these words were far from being the same on Colonel Dermont and Mrs. Verepoint. The lady, though greatly shocked and surprised, believed every word the girl had spoken. The colonel believed none of it.

"Leave the room, and leave the house instantly," he said. "I beg your pardon, Mrs. Verepoint, but I must take the liberty of insisting upon it. I will not have the mind of my young ward exposed to the corruption of this creature. Be gone!" he reiterated with anger. "I will not quit this premises until I know you are out of the way of dear Julia, whose heart she would break if she were allowed to repeat this horrid invention to her."

Susan looked terrified and profoundly miserable, but did not budge. "Oh, sir! Don't send me away!" she cried. "Don't send me away until you are quite, quite sure! Do not let the marriage be until you are quite, quite sure!"

"Do you hear her? Do you hear her insolence, my good lady? I certainly do not choose to lay hands on her myself, but I really must beg, Mrs. Verepoint, that you will permit some of your people to place her outside your gates, if she refuses to go there willingly."

"No sir, no!" said Susan, hastily preparing to leave the room. "I have tried to do my duty by the young gentleman and by you too. Of course, gentlefolk must act as they think right themselves. Perhaps they know better what is right than we do."

Susan wrapped her shawl around her shoulders and humbly curtsied to Mrs. Verepoint before disappearing from the room.

The colonel watched her leave in silence and then turned to the lady of the manor. "Do you think, madam, that since the beginning of the world, there was ever so audacious an instance of falsehood heard?"

"My dear colonel," replied Mrs. Verepoint carefully, "I should indeed be sorry to receive as true a statement which, besides being improbable, makes such a horrible attack on a young lady you must feel so deeply devoted to. Nevertheless, you must forgive me, but if I were in your situation I would not take the improbability of a story as perfect proof against it. I am willing enough to hope that it is, as you suppose, an invention—but this should by no means prevent my inquiring a good deal more about it."

"You may depend upon it, my dear lady, that I will inquire and will do so with no great loss of time. I will now take my leave of you. Give my love to dear little Julia and tell her I shall set the matter of the mortgage right directly. Dear, good little soul! I certainly do love that girl almost as well as if she were my own daughter. She has behaved so beautifully about a little money affair."

Mrs. Verepoint received this praise upon Julia, although it was unintelligible to her.

The colonel continued, "Mrs. Verepoint, will you be so good as to tell me whether you suppose that girl meant to insinuate that Miss Thorwold was married, or was not married, to the Lord William she talked about?"

"I think she meant to say that she was married."

"Now is it not strange," asked the colonel, "that a woman of your excellent judgment should think such a farrago of improbabilities worth inquiring into? Just think it over, will you? Here's a high born lady, niece to a peer of the realm, and united in holy wedlock to a young nobleman. And yet, it is insinuated after running away to London to be married to him, she would run back to the country in order to be married to my son Alfred? I should think it would turn out to be one of the most remarkable cases of bigamy on record! However, I will go and see about it directly."

He gaily kissed her hand and left the room.

On reaching the Mount, he found the family to be in considerable confusion.

"My mistress desired, colonel, that when you came home you would go to her in the housekeeper's room," said a maid servant who was hovering on the steps, waiting for him.

The colonel obeyed without reply and found his lady seated with a large heap of plate spread out on the table before her. The housekeeper and butler, standing side by side, each had a long catalog in their hands. They appeared to be taking account of the valuable articles which lay before them.

"What is all this for, my dear?" asked the colonel. "And why do you want to see me?"

Mrs. Dermont, looking serious and frightened, jumped at the sound of her husband's voice. "Oh, colonel! We have been in such a state since you left us! I am thankful you are home, for I feel as if I did not know what was going to happen next!"

"What is the matter? Where is Alfred? Where is Amelia?" demanded the colonel.

"Oh, poor, dear loves! It was no use plaguing them to come here, so I left them to comfort one another in the library. Poor, dear Amelia! She had the worst fright of all!"

The colonel grew impatient. "I do wish you would tell me exactly what the matter is."

"And so I will, colonel," replied Mrs. Dermont. "We have found out that we have been harboring a most horrid and depraved creature in this house. A thorough paced thief who has been in jail again and again. One of the first things to be thought of was the plate, of course. I was really so anxious about it that I could not be easy until I came here myself. Robinson and Smith are going over it with the catalog."

"If I am not greatly mistaken," returned the colonel, "I could name the girl."

"You don't say, my dear colonel? Then I am sure you have learned something more than we know about her. I am sure she is one of the last girls in the world I should have suspected. It is no other than Susan Jenkins, colonel! Julia Drummond's new maid!"

"To be sure it is, my dear," said the colonel. "Upon my honor and life, I shall think we are very lucky if we escape with only the loss of as much plate as she could carry. I have seen her show off this morning in a style that would prevent my feeling surprised if I saw her set fire to the house. How was she found out here?"

"Why, in the most shocking and abrupt way for poor Miss Thorwold! She was sitting in her own room looking over some of her wedding clothes, when she heard the door open. She looked around saw what frightened her almost out of her senses. It seems she went to London, like an angel as she is, after attending to her dying friend in Nice. It was just in the time she wrote us, you know, she went into lodging for a few days. She knew the woman who kept the lodgings perfectly well, but the poor, good woman had been unlucky enough to take this vile girl, Susan Jenkins, into the house. It was but a day or two before Miss Thorwold left that she was found out to be what she is—a thief and a liar. Well, colonel, you can imagine the shock it must have been to her when she turned her head and saw this horrid creature! She says she believes she screamed, for the girl stepped forward and held her fist in her face, threatening her if she dared to mention ever having seen her before. Miss Thorwold so courageously told her she'd take immediate measures to have her sent from the house, upon which the girl turned around and hurried out. Miss Thorwold came down, frightened out of her senses, and told us what I have now told you. Alfred rang the bell and inquired if Susan Jenkins was still in the house, to which Thomas said no. He said they had seen her rush out with her bonnet and shawl without saying a single word to anybody. That is the whole of the story, colonel."

"The plate seems all right, colonel," said the butler.

"So much the better, Robinson," replied the colonel. "She seems to have started off in too great a hurry to have been able to take much. And now, my dear, if you will come into the drawing room with me, you shall hear what I have to tell of this clever young jail bird. It is no subject for laughter, though. I am truly sorry for her poor father and mother. It is enough to break their hearts."

In the drawing room they found the lovers. Amelia rose shaking from the sofa as the colonel entered, a flash of doom crossing her features. He mistook her agitation as a sign of the fright she had endured, and not for what she feared he might believe. Her worries were cast aside when the colonel pressed a paternal kiss upon her forehead and gallantly led her back to the sofa. He sat himself beside her and began to relate the outrageous tale of the thief, Susan.

"I have no doubt, my dear," he said in conclusion, "that if a sufficient amount of time had allowed her to arrange the facts of her narrative with more attention, Miss Susan Jenkins might become one of the first romancers of the age. But being in a hurry, she rather crowded events upon us. She seemed to forget that she had declared you were married at the beginning, and to be sure, it was altogether the greatest hodge-podge of absurdities. I don't see what we can do to the creature, and that rather vexes me. She ought to be flogged and sent to prison, there is no doubt about that. We cannot punish her for this, or in any other way, you know, without having legal authority for it."

"Upon my word, dear colonel, I think the spectacle of so utterly depraved a young creature is so pitiable, that it is quite unnecessary that the hand of human justice should visit her. The shame to her family and herself is suffering enough."

The beautiful sentiment produced a great effect on the trio who listened to it.

"Angel!" exclaimed Alfred.

"Dear child!" cried Mrs. Dermont. "That is what I call true Christian charity!"

"And so it is, Mrs. Dermont," said the colonel, lifting Amelia's hand to kiss it. "I feel I ought to be ashamed of myself for wishing vengeance upon such a wretch. She is certain of being miserable without any help of mine. God bless you, my dear! You are an example to us all."

# Chapter 23

After the departure of Colonel Dermont, Mrs. Verepoint repeated to her daughter and Miss Drummond all the most essential parts of Susan's terrible narrative. It was not long afterward that a note from Colonel Dermont to Mrs. Verepoint was received, in which he informed her, that the whole mystery of Miss Susan Jenkins' statement had been most satisfactorily explained on his return home. He briefly communicated the leading particulars of Miss Thorwold's experience with Susan.

It was quite in vain that the miserable Julia endeavored to revive Mrs. Verepoint's first prediction in favor of Susan. The excellent lady knew nothing of the girl except for her decent appearance, and the simple style in which she had recounted her narrative. The extreme improbability of the tale made it easier to believe the contradiction rather than the assertion of the facts, and

Mrs. Verepoint believed the contradiction accordingly. She considered it her duty to combat Julia's unjustifiable faith in her servant's wild statement in preference for the perfectly natural explanation of them by a young lady of high birth and consideration. After listening to her reasoning on the subject, Charlotte Verepoint completely joined her mother and Colonel Dermont's view of the case, and Julia was obliged to accept it all.

The days wore themselves away to hours, and the morning fixed for the marriage of Alfred and Amelia arose bright in the autumn sunshine. The little park at the Mount presented a scene of the most pleasing gaiety. Tents were pitched, and a large assemblage of cottagers had been granted permission to lay out their bread and cheese breakfasts on the turf. Abundant supplies of these comforts, accompanied by a liberal allowance of ale, were lodged under the canvas at the earliest hour of the morning.

It had been arranged that the marriage would take place in the parish church at ten, and after the ceremony, a most splendid breakfast table was to receive the brides-folk and their friends in the dining room. The drawing room, with the choicest greenhouse flowers on every table and every stand, was to receive the guests as they arrived. In this room the lovely bride had promised to enter in her bridal array, as soon as she should be informed that the whole company was assembled. Having received the blushing honors which were sure to greet her, Lord Ripley was to lead her to his own carriage, in which she was to be conveyed for the last time as Amelia Thorwold. Alfred's new equipage was sent down from London for the occasion, and was to follow the procession unoccupied, the young man taking his place with his father and mother in the family carriage. When the hands of the happy lovers were united, they would return at the head of the procession together, the road being strewed with flowers by all the young girls in the village—except Susan Jenkins and her sister Nancy.

All the guests had arrived except one—Julia Drummond. It was not necessary for her to feign any excuse for her absence, for having passed a totally sleepless night, she really was too ill in the morning to quit her bed. Mrs. and Miss Verepoint greatly disliked the task of announcing her illness, but with little interest except that she might miss the festivities, Mrs. Dermont simply said, "Ill? Really? How very unlucky!"

A slight murmur was heard from among the crowd of servants assembled in the hall before the drawing room door was thrown open for the bride's reception. With the slow and lingering step of a bashful bride, yet the easy, graceful movements of assured beauty, Amelia Thorwold glided into the room.

Her dress of rich white satin fell around her in folds, while floating over it hung a three-fold tunic of silk gauze. On her head she wore a small, closely woven wreath of orange blossoms mixed with the bright, small leaves of the orange myrtle. A costly veil of the finest Brussels lace attached to the rich coronet of braided hair, which finished her headdress and fell over her whole person. Her face looked out from beneath the delicate cloud, and she stood quietly knowing every pulse was beating high with triumphant pride for her, the beautiful bride.

While Alfred's proper place was in the background, he could not resist the impulse which led him to seize her hand and press it to his lips. He then moved back again, and Amelia accepted the offered arm of her uncle and was led to the carriage which waited for her.

Colonel Dermont gave his arm to Mrs. Knight, who was to occupy the same carriage as Lord Ripley and the bride. Alfred was accompanied by his mother and the fair bridesmaids. The rest of the company had left a moment sooner, everyone feeling the lovely bride must not be kept waiting at the church. Colonel Dermont, having handed everybody in the party into one carriage or another, found he had missed his and the only person left as a companion was a young legal gentleman, sent down by the solicitor who had prepared the settlements. He was to see the settlements properly executed at the conclusion of the wedding ceremony and convey them to their proper strong box at Lord Ripley's solicitors in Lincoln's Inn.

As he was about to enter his carriage, a messenger on a racing horse approached the house. The urgent dispatch he carried was handed to the colonel, who took it without any concern for its contents. He sat opposite the legal professional in the carriage and broke the seal of the letter, grateful for the excuse to be silent with the stranger.

*To Colonel Dermont.*

*Sir,*

*I have been informed on what I fear is extremely good authority, that your son and heir is about to marry—I would say, is about to lead to the altar, a young lady who still calls herself Amelia Thorwold. In fact, she no longer has any right to that name, as on the thirtieth day of last August she was married by banns to the Right Honorable Lord William Hammond, second son of the late Duke of Watertown. That this lady will have rendered herself highly culpable in the eyes of yourself and family, and permitting herself to promise marriage to your son, after living with Lord William for several weeks as his wife, there can be no manner of doubt. I must do her the justice to say that she is, at this moment, of the idea that the ceremony which united her to Lord William Hammond was a fictitious one. The guilt of having thus deceived her must lie at his lordship's door, as may be easily shown, if her lady has preserved the letter which she received from Lord William at my house the day before she left London for your seat at Stoke, called the Mount. That her ladyship has been far from conducting herself properly, I am quite ready to allow, and I assure you, sir, that I am very sorry for it. It is painful for me to feel myself called upon, as I certainly do, to prevent the unpleasant consequences which might accrue to all the parties concerned, were this illegal connection to take place.*

*It is without question that she will derive a degree of satisfaction from knowing herself entitled to the name and rank of Lady William Hammond, and position of sister to the stylish Duke* and Duchess of Watertown, which may, in part, compensate her for the mortification of losing the esteem of your respectable family, and the handsome settlement which a marriage with your son would have assured her. If she does not derive consolation from her name and title, then I know not where she is to look for it, for it is quite certain a more contemptible animal than her husband does not exist. I have been terribly deceived by him myself, but the truth of the whole matter which he revealed to me could not be concealed any longer.

Her husband, Lord William Hammond, is at this time paying his addresses to one Miss Upton Savage, and is likely to be soon engaged to the cruelly deceived young lady. I would beg to submit to Lady William, who I am certain will be shown this communication, that it is her duty to announce to Miss Upton Savage, without delay, the fact of Lord William being already a married man. A notification to the Duke and Duchess of Watertown should also be dispatched as speedily as possible.

Should you, your son, or Lady William herself feel any doubt as to the authenticity of this information, I beg to refer all or any of you to the Reverend Samuel Birdaway, the Rector, who published the banns, and whom I myself saw and heard perform the marriage ceremony, recorded with my signature in the register.

Furthermore, I have included a copy of the certificate of marriage, which I subsequently obtained from the reverend gentleman, and beg to subscribe myself,

Your obedient and humble servant,

*Caroline Stedworth*
*Half Moon Street, Piccadilly*


*P.S. I fear that the money obtained by the young lady to pay her various bills is lost to your family forever.*


The colonel clenched his fists and ground his teeth. The fact that he, his wife, and their worshiped son might be suddenly cast from the highest pinnacle of admiration into a situation so deplorable was a good deal more than he could stand. All the horror, the exposure, the suffering which would've ensued had he not gotten the letter in time, rushed so vividly upon his mind, that instead of sorrow and anger, he felt nothing but thankfulness and joy. He sat for a moment, clasping his hands over his eyes, silently thanking heaven for their deliverance.

"He is not married to her," breathed the colonel.

He opened his eyes to the astonished face of his companion. "I beg your pardon, Mr. Lawrence, for having frightened you, as I am sure I must have done. The violent emotion this letter first gave rise to will be understood once you have read it. Read it, Mr. Lawrence, and I think you will excuse my countenance. A little reflection, however, has turned my anger to thankfulness."

The young man took the letter, and having perused it, said, "You have reasons to be thankful, Colonel Dermont. Though the ceremony could not have bound your son to this unprincipled young woman legally, the having to prove this publicly would have been a very disagreeable business."

"Doubtless, sir, doubtless," replied the colonel. "I feel it is impossible to be too thankful for the timeliness of this letter, though it is not impossible to wish it had been more timely still. But this is ungrateful. Will you, sir, give me the advantage of your advice as to the best mode of making this extraordinary discovery known to the party who are even now entering the church? It will be dreadful for my son, painful to everybody. I even pity the wretched young woman and her uncle, poor man! If he loves her, if he cares for her as the child of his brother, and as bearing the name of his race, his situation must be terrible. For heaven's sake tell me, Mr. Lawrence, to whom had I better first address myself?"

"I think, sir, that in the first instance you should take Lord Ripley aside and put the letter in his own hands. I, if you will give me leave, will prevent the clergyman from placing himself at the altar. I will tell him a letter has reached you which must prevent the performance of the ceremony. To your son, sir, you will of course address him yourself in private, if possible. Perhaps you might be able to lead him to the church porch. For the rest of the company, they will all become acquainted with the facts, somehow or other, in a short space of time."

By the time the young man had finished speaking, the carriage had drawn sufficiently near the church. Colonel Dermont called the servant, who sat beside the coachman, and ordered him to let him out as soon as it stopped. Mr. Lawrence followed.

Lord Ripley, his niece, and Mrs. Knight, together with Mrs. Dermont, Alfred, the bridesmaids, and the clergyman, were already in the vestry. The colonel paused at the door, almost overpowered by the sight of his son, who was radiant with happiness and standing close to his bride.

"Ask Lord Ripley to come out, Lawrence." said the agitated colonel.

His lordship immediately obeyed the summons and with a smiling, full dressed air, he bowed his way past the group in which he stood, and left the vestry.

The colonel waited for him at no great distance, but out of sight of those Lord Ripley had left. When he approached, the colonel took a step forward and, with more dignity than embarrassment, put the document into his lordship's hand.

"May I suggest, Colonel Dermont, that this, whatever it is, should be submitted to my attention after the ceremony? My niece and Mrs. Knight are standing in the vestry, and—"

"I beg your lordship's pardon," the colonel dryly interrupted, "but if your lordship will just look at the document you will see why it needs to be read before the ceremony."

The tone of Colonel Dermont startled him and his color slightly heightened. He turned his eyes upon the letter with more haste, and less elegance, than he generally displayed. As he read, the lips of the peer began to tremble.

"This is an infamous libel, sir!" shot Lord Ripley. He looked fiercely at Colonel Dermont as if determined to call him out. "You cannot possibly put any faith in such a vile and unsubstantiated statement as this. Neither will I believe it possible that you can design to put such an affront upon my niece if you postpone the ceremony. Let me retain this letter, sir, which I will undertake to answer as it deserves by the young lady in the vestry."

"As the letter is addressed to me, Lord Ripley, I must request you return it to my hands. I am, however, willing to return to the vestry with you to undertake an answer."

"Give me leave, sir, to run my eye over this letter once more, and then I will restore it to you," said his lordship.

Colonel Dermont waited patiently while the document was read again.

"This paper asserts that my niece is Lady William Hammond, and sister to the Duke of Watertown," said Lord Ripley, handing the paper back to the colonel. "If this is so, it is quite impossible that I can object to the connection, which is decidedly one of the first in England. There must, I suspect, have been some lover's quarrel between Lord William and his lady, and probably this letter is written at the instigation of his lordship. It is certainly a rather rough mode of winning her back, but it is plain that all Lady William's family can do is make the best of it. I am sure that, in this, you must agree with me, Colonel Dermont."

"Most decidedly, my lord," returned the colonel with something of a smile. "I wish you every success in so laudable an endeavor. It will be desirable, I think, that your lordship should be the one to announce the arrival of this intelligence to the Lady William Hammond, and I think I may venture to undertake the task of consoling my son."

Lord Ripley bowed without making a reply, and walked gracefully towards the vestry, followed by the colonel.

"Thank heaven!" said Alfred as they entered. "Here they come at last."

His lordship appeared to not see any other person present but Mrs. Knight, who he approached and offered his arm. "It is necessary I should speak to you for a few minutes, Mrs. Knight."

The lady was surprised, but took the offered arm.

"I wish you to come with us, Amelia," added his lordship, but without offering his other arm. Upon seeing this, Alfred offered his own, which she took. Lord Ripley stopped immediately and said in perfect nonchalance, "By your leave, Mr. Alfred Dermont, my niece must follow me alone."

Alfred stared at him in surprise, but respectfully obeyed, tenderly pressing the hand he held.

The colonel approached his son and stood for a moment, uncertain of what to do or say. He dreaded the effect of the disclosure he had to make and that so many persons should be present to witness it. He could not leave the little room without risk of encountering the people he was most anxious to avoid, now and forever.

He saw no alternative, and raised his voice to command the attention of all those present. "Will you all, kind friends, forgive the very painful necessity, which will soon be explained to you, will you forgive me if I entreat you to leave me alone with my son and his mother for a few moments?"

Whether they could forgive him or not, for a degree of mystery so exceedingly tormenting, mattered little. The wondering company, bridesmaids and all, were obliged to submit, and in the next moment the young man stood alone between his father and mother.

"My dearest, dearest Alfred, you have a dreadful trial to bear. Let me implore you, for my sake and your mother's, to bear up against it with courage and with moderation in your grief. Read this."

The young man took the letter and retired with it to the window. While his eyes eagerly devoured its contents, the colonel whispered in the ear of his terrified wife, "It is all true, my dear. The whole of Susan's frightful story is true."

The father and mother stood, side by side, their eyes fixed on their adored son, trembling, both of them, in fear they should see him overwhelmed by the fatal tidings.

Alfred read the letter to the end, neither missing a single word nor feeling it necessary to read a single word of it twice. Having finished, he folded it up and walked quietly back towards his parents.

"Why do you both look at me with such fearful anxiety?" he asked. "Is it possible that you can suppose I should feel any touch of sorrow, any particle of regret, at being made acquainted with the disgusting facts communicated by that letter?"

He spoke in a tone much less like that of an outraged, broken hearted lover, and more like that of a high minded man, disdaining what is vile too sincerely to resent it. A spirit of intelligence seemed to have come upon Alfred, and though the visage of his brow was grave, there was an expression of conscious power that gave more triumph than of sorrow to his countenance.

Mrs. Dermont engaged herself in wiping a genuine shower of tears from her eyes. "Alas, my poor, darling Alfred. How will you ever survive the loss of what you so doted on?"

"And alas, my darling mother," replied Alfred, "how vilely I have abused your fond indulgence. How vilely I have yielded myself to all the willfulness of a spoiled child, since all you know of me teaches you to believe that I am likely to die of grief for the loss of such a lady as this. Oh, dearest mother, not only have I been saved from degrading your name by bestowing it for even a moment on this wretched woman, but I have learned what she really is. She has insulted us. She has driven Julia from our home. She has forced the dismissal of our staff and she has played us all for fools. Any trace of affection I felt has been obliterated by these disclosures. After all this, were I to still have any fondness, then I would ask you to weep for me. Cry! But as it is, receive your son again, and you, dear father, take me back, a wiser and better man than when your indulgence permitted me to risk so desperate a stake for this unknown toy."

As he spoke, he extended a hand to each parent with an aspect so full of hope and thankfulness, their fears and sorrows immediately changed to rejoicing—until they remembered the awkward position of their guests. A strange sort of dismissal was impossible, especially as many were staying at the Mount.

"Upon my word," said Mrs. Dermont. "I do not know what to do."

"Let them go back to the Mount for breakfast," said Alfred. "Let the whole party do so. It would be in poor taste for me to display myself before them, nor would it be well for me to do the honors of a bridal breakfast when the bride has so decidedly given herself to another. But I see no reason why you should insist upon sending the company away starving."

"Well, dearest Alfred, I believe you are right," returned the colonel. He was greatly relieved to be spared from the necessity of telling his friends and family that they were all expected to take themselves off as fast as possible.

They all three began to depart when Alfred laid a hand upon his father's arm to detain him. "I wish, sir, that you would tell Mrs. Verepoint that I should consider it a great act of kindness if she could go home directly, and take me with her. She will understand, I am sure, that it would be disagreeable for me to return to the Mount just now."

"Certainly, my dear fellow. No doubt of it," replied the colonel.

The party returning to the Mount lost no time in replacing themselves in their carriages. When they had fairly driven out of sight, the deserted bridegroom came forth from the vestry, and without speaking a word to either, offered an arm to Mrs. Verepoint and her daughter. He led them to their carriage, which was now the only one of the brilliant cortege which remained standing before the forsaken church.

# Chapter 24

Not a word had been uttered during the ride to the Grange, and the first Alfred spoke after handing Mrs. and Miss Verepoint down from the carriage were, "Will you have the kindness to tell Miss Drummond that I should like to speak with her?"

It was evident the young man would be more at ease without their society, and the mother and daughter retired together. They were by no means displeased at being dismissed, for though neither were particularly interested in gossip, they could not help but feel a little impatient to tell Julia the events of the morning.

Alfred was relieved to find himself standing alone when they left. He wished for leisure and solitude to let his mind rest. Instead, he was tortured by how he had treated dear Julia. Innocent Julia, a million times too pure to accept the vileness of Amelia, but too kind to say a single word against her. And then came other thoughts. His father had told him she refused to say that *she did not love the person to whom she had lent the money*. He remembered also the prompt refusal of young Borrowdale. He pushed it from his mind completely. With all the emotions he had encountered in the short span of a few hours, he could not form a rational thought now. All he hoped in the moment, all he wished, was that she would be generous enough to restore him to that dear and precious niche in her young heart.

Mrs. and Miss Verepoint, meanwhile, hastened to the apartment of Julia, where they found her engaged in sealing a letter. She looked rather surprised at seeing them so soon returned, and colored as she looked from one to the other, expecting them to describe the splendid ceremony.

"Are you tolerably firm in the nerves, Julia?" asked Miss Verepoint.

"Why would you ask me that, Charlotte? I do not think you have anything to tell me likely to shake my nerves."

"Prepare yourself, dear child," said Mrs. Verepoint. "Your nerves will not likely stand the history we bring you, unmoved."

"What do you mean? Has anything happened to Susan?"

"Susan?" repeated the old lady. "We have seen no more of Susan, poor girl. But we have found out about her, Julia, that she told the truth—although she by no means knew all of the story she undertook to tell."

Julia pressed both hands against her heart. "Is any of it proved?"

"Yes, my dear," replied Mrs. Verepoint. "It is all proved and a great deal more."

"And Alfred?"

"Well, I think Alfred is as well as can be expected," said Charlotte.

Julia's face grew pale from the agony of doubt. "He is not married to her?"

"No, my dear, he is not married to her," said Mrs. Verepoint. "You need not look so terrified. At any rate, there was no danger of him being really married to her because she is already married to another. And then, fancy her having persuaded poor Alfred to pay her debts! There is a degree of depravity in the whole history that is really just too painful to think of."

"Julia has not yet had the message with which we came charged, mama," said Charlotte. "The bachelor bridegroom has come home with us, Julia, in order to avoid the rather queer style of congratulation which, perhaps, he expected at the Mount, where, as you know, there is an immense gathering which could not be dispersed at the moment. Those who were not at the church still expected a breakfast. Our message is from Alfred, my dear, who desired us to say he very greatly wished to see you."

Julia grew still. "Indeed, I cannot see him. I suppose he may wish to say something to me, to make some apology about poor Susan. To tell you the truth, I would rather not talk about it, for I do not think she was well treated."

"But is that reason enough for your refusing to see an old friend?" asked Charlotte. "And at such a moment, too?"

Julia sighed. "No, it is not. I ought to see him, for I wish to send a message to my guardian."

The three ladies descended the stairs together, and found Alfred walking in long strides up and down the library. His face lit up when he saw her.

Julia remained calm and cool, although the sight of him and the weight of the news she'd just received made her feel faint.

"Shall we leave you two to converse privately?" asked Mrs. Verepoint.

"No," replied Julia kindly. "Please stay."

"Mrs. Verepoint," said Alfred, "there is nothing I can say now that you do not already know."

Alfred began by disclosing the details of the letter to Julia, and how so many things he had overlooked should have been so obvious. He expressed frankly how he might have prevented it all if only he had not been prevented by preposterous folly to look deeper than the fair surface, while his fit of love lasted. Julia listened to him, unmoved, as he detailed his ardent thankfulness for his escape. She listened in perfect silence and nothing in her eyes, at any time, expressed any interest in what was passing. Both Mrs. Verepoint and Charlotte believed that, with more resentment than they thought natural to her, she was still thinking of the unceremonious dismissal of her favorite, Susan. It appeared Alfred thought so too, for after suffering severely from her cold silence, he suddenly said, "I hope, my dear Julia, that your poor Susan will forgive our abominable behavior to her, and that she will come back to you immediately. Do you think she can forgive us, Julia?"

"She is a good hearted and intelligent girl, Alfred, and is too grateful to your parents for all their kindness towards her family, to permit her being conscious of any feeling like resentment."

"And she will return to you immediately, will she not?" he asked.

"I have no doubt of it," replied Julia, who then relapsed again into silence.

While it appeared to be missed by everyone else, it did not escape Julia's notice that Alfred had not once addressed, or apologized for, any injury done to her.

All the neighborhood was gossiping about the extraordinary discovery of Lady William Hammond's previous marriage. Within a short time after the wild event of Alfred's non-wedding, Julia Drummond departed for Scotland. Colonel Dermont, Mrs. Dermont, and Alfred were slow to recover from their astonishment upon finding that the young lady had arranged everything for her trip. On the morning of the wedding ceremony that never was, Julia accepted the regularly repeated invitation of her nearest surviving relative, Mrs. MacKensie, and fixed the date for her arrival.

Alfred was lost as to the cause of her taking so extraordinary a resolution at such a time. It was difficult for him to pinpoint the precise moment after accepting he was no longer a bound man that he had found, in her absence—at the bottom of his heart—a hidden pearl of affection for his childhood friend. The interval between his hope of becoming the husband of Amelia, and his hope of becoming the husband of Julia, was not very long.

After the lamentable blunders which he had fallen into, he was lost as to how likely Julia would be to agree with him on the subject of matrimony. He dared not speculate on the memories that nestled around his heart. After he had endured the dreary blank which her absence made for more than a month, he informed his father and mother that, with their permission, he intended to ask Julia Drummond if she could forgive the folly and all the consequences of his first choice, and become his wife.

Colonel and Mrs. Dermont were quick to recount her numerous virtues. They acknowledged that Julia had grown tall and handsome. She had refused the son, and probably the heir, of a peer. She was of age, and in possession of her little fortune. She had been right about Susan, when they had all been wrong. And last, although by no means least, she had found the means to withdraw herself from the matchless Mount, and send word that she was very well and exceedingly happy. Young as she was, there was something about her character that offered an agreeable contrast to the terrific matron that had crossed their path in the shape of a young lady of fashion.

The father and mother looked at each other with a smile as they listened to this new proposal from their son.

"Well, my dear boy," said the colonel, "I do not have any objection at all, I confess. What do you say, my dear?"

"Really, colonel, considering what we have seen of the conduct of beautiful young ladies whom we did not know well enough to judge thoroughly, I confess, I am inclined to see the wisdom in Alfred's marrying little Julia. More than inclined, actually. I am grateful he should take such a lovely girl over urging him to set off upon another fresh chase of strangers."

Thus sanctioned, Alfred sat down to write the friend of his whole life, the dear companion whose value he had only discovered once he had lost her. He wrote that if she would consent to be his wife, he would consent to be her pupil evermore. If she would not grow weary of teaching, he would not grow weary of learning—in the hope that he might, in time, be more worthy to approach her as an equal. An equal he could never be until she consented to become his loved and lovely instructor, and his compassionate guardian angel through life.

The charming letter, full of truth and feeling, reached its destination safely. It was the third letter Julia had received from Alfred since her arrival at Eagle's Cliff, the two former having both been long and affectionate. Her reply to the first was reserved, though kind, and by no means as long as his own. The second she had not replied to at all.

Since this was written before a reply to the last had even been received, when Julia opened this third letter she felt certain that it contained something more important than its predecessors. She decided not to read it in the presence of her pleasant old aunt, getting up quietly, and taking it to her room. She seated herself in a comfortable, high backed chair and read Alfred's letter. The tears as she read were fast and full.

Alfred had clearly spent many hours rehearsing to himself little passages of their past lives, and Julia, being the best informed of the two on the subject, had come to the realization that, again and again, she had betrayed her feelings to him.

Before she went to bed that night she wrote a reply, not more than an eighth as long as his had been, where she gently, gratefully, meekly—but most decidedly—declined his offered hand. Then, breathing one deep sigh, she sealed her dispatch.

"No, my dearest Alfred," she said to herself. "You will not make a shipwreck of your happiness again by mistaking your heart a second time. You have found out that admiration is not love, nor is pity, either. I am not weak and wicked enough to do that to you."

The effect of this reply upon the unfortunate Alfred was dire. His pride, self esteem, and his confidence in the affection of all who approached him had already been trampled down to dust by his adventure with the worthless Amelia.

For many hours Alfred hid himself from all eyes. Finally, his resolution taken, he sought his parents with Julia's letter open in his hand. The astonishment they felt as he read Julia's words back to them was immense.

The colonel placed a hand gently on the shoulder of his son. "What now, my dear boy?"

"My only wish now is to leave England," Alfred said.

"Do you wish to go alone?" Mrs. Dermont asked.

"No," he replied. "I want you both to accompany me, but on the condition that Julia's name not be mentioned between us. My heart could not bear it."

Alfred knew the heart of Julia had been bruised in their presence by the insinuating spirit of the hateful Amelia. He had seen it and adored that Amelia still. He dared hope Julia would someday forgive it, but could not hear her lovely name until the time would come that she did.

# Chapter 25

For four long years the devoted family, leaving behind the Mount, wandered over nearly the whole of Europe. Alfred could not return to the house where he and Julia had grown up and lived together in such sweet union, and so the interval was not lost, or useless. He never conquered his remorse for the folly that had lost her, but neither did he allow it to conquer him.

It was only the sudden death of a principle tenant on their estate that made a return to Stoke absolutely necessary. When the choice of remaining abroad or returning to England was offered to Alfred, he consented to return. He did not, however, agree to go to the Mount and, instead, remained in London. The colonel and Mrs. Dermont, both longing to see their home, proceeded to Stoke without him.

Meanwhile, Julia had found a dearly maternal friend and a tranquil home at Eagle's cliff. She had a fine old library there, and the young Miss Drummond continued to grow rapidly into a studious woman.

Mrs. MacKensie's only daughter, who was married to a wealthy Scotch baronet, invited Julia to accompany their family to London for a few weeks. Julia was not tempted to go because she did not fancy she should like London, but Mrs. MacKensie insisted that she should have a proper season. Within a week of the acceptance being made on her behalf, Julia found herself a guest at their London home in Grosvenor Place.

Sir James and Lady Bruce had a large circle of acquaintance, and Julia was far from amused at the variety of new scenes to which she was introduced. Ball followed ball in rapid succession. Julia, though sometimes weary, yielded to the wishes of her hostess. She was attired in fine dresses and went many a night with little sleep, all without grumbling. She took it all in perfect stride, until a trouble came upon her which made her look forward with a great deal of impatience to their return home.

Julia, who had grown into absolute loveliness, and who had speedily become one of the acknowledged beauties of the season, received an offer of marriage from one Lord Eton. This raised the triumph of her obliging friends to the highest pitch, and the more Julia persisted in assuring his lordship she could not do herself the honor of accepting him, the more they privately assured him that her refusal was just youthful shyness.

All this had gone on for a week or two when matters were brought to a conclusion in an unexpected manner. Lord Eton had determined that his fate with the fair one, at whose feet he was willing to lay both his coronet and himself forever, would be decided at a ball where he knew he would meet her.

Having screwed his courage firmly at this resolution, he stood ready to receive her at the entrance. He engaged her to dance, presented his arm, and instead led her to a small room prepared for chess and flirtation. She was relieved to have a modicum of privacy with him, for she, too, thought it was time to convince his lordship once and for all that she was in earnest.

He placed her on a sofa and seated himself in a chair opposite her. In a manner equally sincere and respectful, he began to repeat his humble hope that time, and a conviction of his devoted love, might operate in his favor.

There was at first a restless impatience in her eye, expressing a wish that he go on and finish so she might answer him. Then, her eye became fixed, and there was an anxious uncertainty in its expression which he could not comprehend. He pursued his theme and asked her to give him an answer.

"I beg your pardon, my lord—what have you been saying, sir?" she stammered.

Lord Eton followed his eyes to the direction hers had just been in. On the opposite side of the small room stood a figure that he guessed might have fixed the eye of any lady in the world. A strikingly handsome young man, considerably above the common height, leaned against the frame of the door with peculiar dignity and grace. A single glance sufficed to show that he was as completely engaged in gazing at Miss Drummond as she was at him.

"Julia! Miss Drummond!" Lord Eton said in a low voice. "Answer me, I beg of you. I have placed my honor, my happiness, almost my life in your hands. In return, I only ask to know your will. Julia, is there any hope for me? May I ever hope that you will be my wife?"

"Never, never," replied Julia. She was gentle as always, but with a decisiveness of tone that made it impossible for him to mistake her.

Lord Eton looked at her earnestly for a moment, and then took her hand and kissed it.

"God bless you and wish you happy, Julia," he said politely, before standing and passing through the door nearest the sofa.

As soon as he was gone, Alfred sprung forward. "Julia Drummond! So exquisite, yet ever, ever the same! Who was that?"

"That was Lord Eton," replied Julia. Her heart raced.

"What right had he to use your Christian name? And what was it you told him could never, never be?"

Alfred Dermont was vastly improved in many ways since they had parted last, but at that moment Julia had no reason to believe he had conquered his impetuosity. Not only did he speak with an intensity she didn't feel he had right to, but his eyes turned to the door which the discarded nobleman had made his exit.

"I have bid my final farewell to Lord Eton. You need not concern yourself with him," she said.

"Nay, Julia," Alfred replied in a softened tone, "I was only concerning myself with you."

"He can never be anything to me," she replied, composed and cool. "You heard me tell him so."

"And you have told me the same, Julia," returned Alfred. "I hope he will not dwell for lingering years upon the words with the same misery that I have done."

He dropped into the chair that Lord Eton had occupied, and neither uttered a word. Julia heard the beating of her own heart and was horribly afraid that he might hear it also.

Alfred leaned forward and tenderly took her hand. "Julia, for more than four years I have believed the letter you wrote to me from Eagle's Cliff had sealed my fate forever. I cannot, Julia—*I cannot*—guess why it is I should be mad enough to risk the agony of another refusal. But, were I to ask the same question of you that I presume that unhappy young man asked—if once more I were to ask you to be my wife—Julia, my dear Julia, would you repeat your 'Never, never?'"

Julia's eyes were fixed upon the carpet as he spoke. When he had quite stopped, she raised her eyes and met his. "Would I give you the same answer I gave Lord Eton? Would I, four years later, give you, dear Alfred, the same answer I gave you in that letter?"

She smiled at the man she had loved her whole life and replied, "Never, never."

## The End

# Acknowledgments

I have to start by thanking the prolific English novelist, Mrs. Frances Milton Trollope, for writing Young Love and an extraordinary compilation of work that totals over one hundred titled volumes.

Thank you to the British Library and the archive preservation efforts of the University of Illinois at Urbana-Champaign.

I am always and forever grateful to Ashar, my husband, who indulges and spoils me far beyond what is acceptable practice towards even the best of wives.

My inspiration and desire to work with wholesome manuscripts comes from the children who have touched my soul: Alishba, Cora, Luke, Sienna, Calla, and Juniper.

My love of all things Georgian, Regency, and Victorian was inherited from my mother, who I miss dearly.

My passion for living life to its fullest comes from Daddy, who I love with ever fiber of my being. You are the center –the very heart—of my universe.

My encouragement to write comes from my mentor and friend, Bonnie Hearn Hill. Thank you for giving me the courage to actually finish something.

Finally, hats off to all the rest of my family and friends for your continued love and support.